男孩女孩的

THE GREEN ROOM

夏日劇場學園

Robert Campbell 著

安卡斯 譯

ABOUT THIS BOOK

For the Student

🎧 Listen to the story and do some activities on your Audio CD.

💬 Talk about the story.

⭐ Prepare for Cambridge English: Preliminary (PET) for schools

For the Teacher

HELBLING e·ZONE THE EDUCATIONAL PLATFORM A state-of-the-art interactive learning environment with 1000s of free online self-correcting activities for your chosen readers.

Go to our Readers Resource site for information on using readers and downloadable Resource Sheets, photocopiable Worksheets, and Tapescripts. www.helblingreaders.com

For lots of great ideas on using Graded Readers consult Reading Matters, the Teacher's Guide to using Helbling Readers.

Level 4 Structures

Sequencing of future tenses	Could / was able to / managed to
Present perfect plus *yet, already, just*	Had to / didn't have to
First conditional	Shall / could for offers
Present and past passive	May / can / could for permission Might for future possibility
How long?	Make and let
Very / really / quite	Causative have Want / ask / tell someone to do something

Structures from lower levels are also included.

CONTENTS

Hi, Robert, can you tell us a little about yourself?

I was born in Wales, grew up in Scotland, and then lived in England for many years. Now I live in Spain where I spend most of my time writing. This is the third reader I've written for Helbling Languages.

Where did you get the idea for this story?

The Green Room is about some young people at a summer theater school. When I was a teenager, I wanted to be an actor so I joined the National Youth theater (NYT). The NYT is an organization that encourages[1] young people aged 14-21 to learn about the theater. A lot of actors have been members including Orlando Bloom, Daniel Craig, Daniel Day-Lewis, Helen Mirren, and Matt Smith.

The first play[2] I acted[3] in was *Zigger Zagger* which was about football fans[4]. It was an amazing[5] experience so I decided to write a story about teenagers having a similar experience today.

Did you ever become a professional[6] actor?

No, I wasn't good enough! But a few years later I wrote the music for some NYT plays and became a musical[7] director[8]. I wrote the music and songs for a lot of shows before I started writing stories. One of the shows was about the actor James Dean, who is mentioned in the story.

Does the story have a message?

Yes, it does. But you'll have to read the story to find out what the message is.

---

encourage [ɪnˈkɝɪdʒ] (v.) 鼓舞
play [ple] (n.) 戲劇
act [ækt] (v.) 演出
fan [fæn] (n.) 迷；紛絲
amazing [əˈmezɪŋ] (a.) 驚人的
professional [prəˈfɛʃənl] (a.) 職業的
musical [ˈmjuzɪkl̩] (a.) 配樂的
director [dəˈrɛktɚ] (n.) 指導人

1 Look at the pictures of the main characters in the story and write the correct name in each sentence.

Laura   Lucy   Marc   Nathan

a .... is ambitious and likes wearing bright colors.

b .... is quite shy and wears glasses.

c .... is romantic and has long hair.

d .... is ambitious and has fair hair.

2 Which of the characters do you think likes drawing? Give a reason for your answer.

3 Choose one of the characters and imagine you are him/her. Think about what "you" are like. Write down adjectives to describe yourself, hobbies, friends, etc.

Now in pairs introduce yourselves. Ask and answer questions. See how much information you can find out about the other character.

4 One of the settings of *The Green Room* is inside a theater. Label the pictures with these theater words.

a	audience	people who watch a show
b	auditorium	part of a theater where the public sits
c	costumes	clothes actors wear in a play
d	foyer	area near the entrance of a theater
e	rehearsal room	place where actors and musicians practice
f	scenery	objects and backgrounds that represent the location of a play
g	stage	part of a theater where the actors perform
h	wings	area at each side of the stage that the public doesn't see

5 The "green room" is another place in a theater. What do you think it is?

—— a a room where actors change into their costumes

—— b a place where actors can relax

—— c a box where some of the audience sits

6 Read the advertisement and answer the questions.

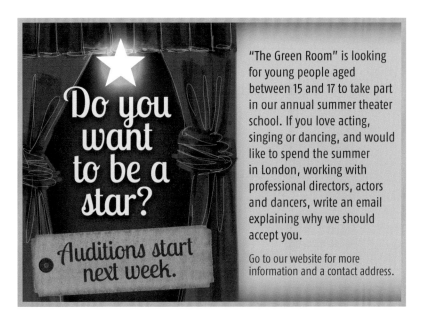

Do you want to be a star?

Auditions start next week.

"The Green Room" is looking for young people aged between 15 and 17 to take part in our annual summer theater school. If you love acting, singing or dancing, and would like to spend the summer in London, working with professional directors, actors and dancers, write an email explaining why we should accept you.

Go to our website for more information and a contact address.

a Are you the right age to attend "The Green Room" summer school?

b Which area are you most interested in—acting, singing, or dancing?

c Would you like to do the course? Why or why not?

d "Auditions start next week." What are auditions? How do you say the word in your language?

7 Write an email to "The Green Room" saying why you want to take part in the summer school.

To:	auditions@thegreenroom.com
From:	
Subject:	Auditions for "The Green Room" summer school

8 William Shakespeare (Will) and James Dean (James) both feature in the story. What do you know about them? Circle the correct name.

William Shakespeare   James Dean

Will James ⓐ He wrote around 38 theater plays.

Will James ⓑ He was an actor.

Will James ⓒ He was English.

Will James ⓓ He only made three films.

Will James ⓔ He was born in 1564.

Will James ⓕ He died in 1955.

Will James ⓖ He was called the first American teenager.

Will James ⓗ His famous quotes include: "If music be the food of love, play on."

9 Use the words in the box to complete the titles of some of Shakespeare's plays.

> Dream   Errors   It   Juliet
> Night   Nothing   Venice   Well

- a   All's Well That Ends _____
- b   As You Like _____
- c   The Comedy of _____
- d   The Merchant of _____
- e   A Midsummer Night's _____
- f   Much Ado about _____
- g   Romeo and _____
- h   Twelfth _____

10 Look at some of Marc's drawings from the story. What can you see in the pictures? What do you think happens in the story?

11 Read and listen to this text about a play. Then read the sentences below and tick (✓) true (T) or false (F).

The students at "The Green Room" summer school come together to produce a play. A play has many different elements to it. A play has a plot. The plot of a play is usually based on dialogue, which is what the characters say. A play also has stage directions, which are written instructions given by the playwright. The stage directions give information about the setting of the play. The setting is where and when the play takes place, helped also by the scenery. The stage directions also help the actors understand how to move and act.

T F ⓐ A play doesn't have a plot.
T F ⓑ Stage directions are written instructions.
T F ⓒ The setting of a play is helped by scenery.
T F ⓓ Stage directions are only about the setting of a play.

"What am I doing here?" Laura asked herself, looking over the shoulder of the boy in front of her. There was a long line of teenagers standing outside the theater [2] and Laura was at the end of the queue [3].

"There are at least eighty people here," she thought.

It was Saturday morning and Laura was feeling nervous as she waited to go inside the theater. She was also feeling guilty [4] because she had lied to Mum and Dad at breakfast.

"Where are you going?" Dad asked.

"To Lucy's house," Laura said. "We have to revise [5] for an exam and then we have swimming practice."

"Will you be late?" Mum asked.

"I don't know. I'll phone. OK?"

Lucy knew about the plan in case [6] Laura's mum or dad phoned her. Lucy was Laura's best friend and she always helped Laura out [7].

When Laura left home in the morning, carrying her sports bag, she started walking in the direction of Lucy's house but when she reached [8] the main road, she turned left instead of right and walked quickly to the train station. There was a train at 10:03 and the journey [9] to London only took 30 minutes. She could easily reach the theater before 11:00.

---

1 audition [ɔˋdɪʃən] (n.) 試演
2 theater [ˋθɪətɚ] (n.) 劇場
3 queue [kju] (n.) 排成行列
4 guilty [ˋgɪltɪ] (a.) 內疚的
5 revise [rɪˋvaɪz] (v.) 〔英〕復習

6 in case 萬一
7 help out 幫助擺脫困境
8 reach [ritʃ] (v.) 抵達
9 journey [ˋdʒɝnɪ] (n.) 車程時間

On the train, she took her sports bag[1] to the toilet and changed clothes—a red top[2] to attract[3] attention, her best jeans, and the new shoes she bought with Lucy last weekend. She put on some make-up[4] and then looked at herself in the mirror. "You can do it!" she told herself.

Laura felt so confident[5] on the train but now she was standing outside the theater and she felt nervous and guilty.

"What am I doing here?" she asked again. But this time she realized[6] she said it aloud because the boy in front turned round and looked at her.

"Are you talking to me?" said the boy in glasses.

Now Laura was feeling nervous, guilty *and* stupid. She wanted to run back to King's Cross station and take the first train home. But then she saw the notebook in the boy's hand. He was drawing a picture of the queue of teenagers standing outside the theater.

Laura smiled.

"That's a really good drawing[7]," she said.

"Thanks," he said.

"I'm Laura," she said.

"I'm Marc," the boy said. "Marc with a c. Like Marc Chagall."

When Laura didn't react, Marc added, "The painter[8]?"

"I know who Marc Chagall is," Laura lied.

Marc smiled and Laura felt positive[9] again.

"He believed me," she thought. "Maybe I really am a good actor."

1 sports bag 運動包包 2 top 上衣
3 attract [ə`trækt] (v.) 吸引
4 make-up [`mek,ʌp] (n.) 化妝品
5 confident [`kɑnfədənt] (a.) 有信心的

6 realize [`rɪə,laɪz] (v.) 了解到
7 drawing [`drɔɪŋ] (n.) 鉛筆畫
8 painter [`pentɚ] (n.) 畫家
9 positive [`pɑzətɪv] (a.) 正面的；
　有自信的

The doors finally opened at 11:05 and the teenagers started walking into the theater.

Nathan, who was near the front of the queue, looked around him, trying to see Marc. Where was he? They agreed to meet at the theater but Nathan couldn't see him.

Inside the theater auditorium[1], Nathan sat down in the front row and breathed in deeply. He loved the smell of the theater. Every time he visited a theater, he had the same feeling. It was a difficult feeling to describe[2]. It was like coming home after being away for a long time. For Nathan, this was the most exciting place in the world. Anything could happen here.

After a few minutes, a woman walked onto the stage and everyone started applauding[3]. It was Dame[4] Helen, director of "The Green Room", and one of the country's most famous actors. She raised her hand and suddenly there was silence.

"Thank you for coming to audition for 'The Green Room' summer school theater," she said. "As I'm sure you know, each year we audition hundreds of young people between the ages of fifteen and seventeen from all around the country. If you are successful today then you will spend your summer holidays here in London, working with professional directors, actors and musicians. You will learn about acting[5], dancing and singing, and you will perform in this year's production[6] in this theater, on this stage, in front of a real audience[7]."

Audition

- What are the teenagers auditioning for?
- Have you ever been to an audition?
- Do you think auditions make you feel nervous?

For a moment, Nathan could see himself standing on the stage next to Dame Helen, performing in front of hundreds of people.

"Over the years," Dame Helen continued, "many of today's most successful theater, film and music stars have started their careers[8] here, sitting where you are sitting now, and waiting nervously for their first audition."

Dame Helen paused[9] for a moment and Nathan was sure she smiled at him.

"An audition is like meeting someone for the first time," she said. "You want to make a good impression but it's not always possible. We're all different. If you aren't lucky this time, then don't give up hope. Learn from the experience and believe in yourself. Good luck."

Dame Helen smiled and everyone applauded and cheered[10] as she left the stage.

Then four assistants[11] appeared and divided everyone into four groups. The groups were taken to different parts of the theater.

Nathan followed his group out of the auditorium, down a corridor[12] and up a staircase[13] that twisted[14] and turned all the way up to the very top of the building where there was a big metal door with a "No Entry[15]" sign on it.

"This is it," he thought as he walked through the door.

---

1 auditorium [ˌɔdəˈtorɪəm] (n.) 觀眾席
2 describe [dɪˈskraɪb] (v.) 描述
3 applaud [əˈplɔd] (v.) 鼓掌
4 Dame [dem] (n.)（用來專指具某特殊身分的）女性頭銜
5 acting [ˈæktɪŋ] (n.) 演戲
6 production [prəˈdʌkʃən] (n.) 藝術作品
7 audience [ˈɔdɪəns] (n.) 觀眾

8 career [kəˈrɪr] (n.) 職業生涯
9 pause [pɔz] (v.) 暫停
10 cheer [tʃɪr] (v.) 歡呼
11 assistant [əˈsɪstənt] (n.) 助理
12 corridor [ˈkɔrɪdɚ] (n.) 走廊
13 staircase [ˈstɛrˌkes] (n.) 樓梯
14 twist [twɪst] (v.) 旋轉
15 entry [ˈɛntrɪ] (n.) 進入

In another part of the theater, Marc was standing in a large crowded¹ room. A young man with red hair and a red beard was standing on a chair.

"Listen, everyone!" said the young man. "Find some space² on the floor and sit down."

Marc chose a space at the back of the room and sat down with his back against the wall. The room was bare³ apart from⁴ some tall mirrors on one wall. Marc put on his glasses and looked around for Nathan but he couldn't see him. Maybe he was with one of the other groups in another part of the theater. Then he saw Laura sitting in the middle of the room. He waved to her but she didn't see him.

The red-haired man clapped⁵ his hands to attract everyone's attention.

"Listen, everyone!" he said, "My name is Bob." He waited for everyone to be quiet and then he continued, "First, I want each of you to stand up and tell the rest of us who you are and why you are here."

Marc tried to be invisible⁶. He didn't like talking about himself. He took out his notebook and started to draw a picture of the first person who stood up. She was a fifteen-year-old girl and her name was Jan. She was there because she wanted to be a dancer more than anything in the whole world⁷. Marc could see how nervous the girl was because of the way she stood with her hands together, her eyes looking at the floor.

1 crowded [ˈkraʊdɪd] (a.) 擁擠的
2 space [spes] (n.) 空間
3 bare [bɛr] (a.) 沒有任何陳設的
4 apart from 除了⋯⋯之外
5 clap [klæp] (v.) 拍手
6 invisible [ɪnˈvɪzəbl] (a.) 不會被看到的
7 more than anything in the whole
 world 勝於世上的其他所有一切

Then Laura stood up. She was more confident than Jan. First, she looked straight into Bob's eyes and then at all the people around her. After waiting a few seconds, she started speaking.

"My name is Laura. I live with my mother in Pinewood. My father's dead. We live in Pinewood to be near the film studio[1]. I'm here because I want to be a famous actor like my mother."

Everyone was suddenly[2] interested in Laura.

"Who is your mother?" Bob asked Laura.

"I'd prefer not to say," Laura said.

Confidence[3]

- How is Laura more confident than Jan?
- Are you confident?
- Do you think confidence is important?

Bob smiled and nodded[4]. A boy stood up and introduced himself. Soon all the other people in the room took it in turn to stand up and introduce themselves until there was just one person left.

"And who are you?" Bob asked.

Marc got nervously to his feet[5].

"I'm Marc," he said quietly.

"And why are you here, Marc?" Bob asked.

"Because Nathan told me to come," Marc said.

Everyone in the room started laughing. Marc felt his face burning red. He looked at Laura. She was laughing too.

"And do you do everything that Nathan tells you to do?" Bob asked.

Bob walked over to where Marc was standing and took the notebook from him. He started turning the pages of the notebook, looking at the drawings.

"These are good. Where did you learn to draw?" Bob asked.

"I taught myself," Marc said.

Bob nodded his head, then clapped his hands and spoke loudly.

"OK, everyone! I want you to get into groups of three. I'm going to give you a situation and I want you to prepare a scene[6] to perform for Dame Helen. OK?"

1 film studio 電影製片廠
2 suddenly [ˋsʌdn̩lɪ] (adv.) 突然地
3 confidence [ˋkɑnfədəns] (n.) 信心
4 nod [nɑd] (v.) 點頭
5 get to one's feet 站起身來
6 scene [sin] (n.) 場景

4 Nathan

In the room at the top of the theater, Nathan was with his group, performing his audition for Dame Helen. For the audition scene, he was acting with a girl. They had to improvise[1] a scene in which they were a mother and father, arguing[2] about their teenage daughter. It was eleven o'clock in the evening and the mother and father were waiting for their daughter to come home.

Nathan wasn't sure how to start but the girl knew exactly what to say.

"I'm the one who always has to clean up[3] the mess[4]," she said angrily to Nathan.

"What do you mean?" Nathan asked. He was surprised. The girl sounded and acted like a real mother. The girl continued.

"You work all day. You come home and fall asleep in front of the television. You don't talk to me and you never talk to your daughter!"

"That's not true," Nathan said.

"Did you talk to her when she played truant[5] from school?" the girl said. "Did you talk to her when the police brought her home? When did you last talk to her?"

Nathan didn't know what to say. He opened his mouth but no words came out. Luckily, everyone thought he was acting. Then he had an idea.

"The problem is that you talk too much," he said. "You never know when to stop. You always criticize[6] her and tell her what not to do and where not to go and what not to wear and who not to see. You need to give her some space to breathe. You need to give both of us some space!"

There was a pause. Then the girl spoke.

"I'll talk to her when she comes home," she said.

"No!" Nathan shouted.

Everyone in the room applauded at the end of the scene and Dame Helen smiled and said, "Well done!"

Nathan sat down with the girl. He was shaking with excitement.

"You were amazing," he said to the girl. "You were *so* real."

"Thanks," the girl said. "You weren't bad either." A buzzing[7] sound was coming from her bag. She took out her phone and read a message[8]. She looked worried.

"Is everything OK?" Nathan asked.

"Yeah," she said. "It's a message from my best friend. She doesn't know I'm here. I don't think she's going to be happy when she finds out."

1 improvise [ˈɪmprəvaɪz] (v.) 即席表演
2 argue [ˈɑrgju] (v.) 爭吵；爭論
3 clean up 收拾
4 mess [mɛs] (n.) 混亂；困境
5 truant [ˈtruənt] (n.) 逃學者
6 criticize [ˈkrɪtɪˌsaɪz] (v.) 批評
7 buzzing [ˈbʌzɪŋ] (a.) 嗡嗡作響的
8 message [ˈmɛsɪdʒ] (n.) 手機簡訊

At the end of the audition, Laura sent a text message to her best friend, Lucy, "All cool. CU¹ soon," she wrote. The audition went well. Laura made an impression by talking about her famous mother, and Bob and Dame Helen liked her audition scene. As she followed Marc and the others down the corridor, she could feel people looking at her and she heard someone say, "Who do you think her mother is?"

In the theater foyer², all the teenagers were talking about the auditions and laughing and joking. Laura took out her phone to read Lucy's reply³ to her message. "CU sooner than you think!"

At first, Laura didn't understand the message. But then she looked across the foyer and saw a familiar⁴ face. She walked quickly through the crowd to where Nathan was standing with the girl from his audition scene.

"Lucy! What are you doing here?" Laura asked the girl.

Lucy didn't know what to say. Then she smiled nervously.

"Hi Laura," she said.

"Lucy? What are you doing here?" Laura repeated.

"I was jealous⁵," Lucy said. "You are always talking about the auditions. I wanted to come for myself." She turned to Nathan and said, "See? She's not happy, is she?"

Marc walked over to where they were all standing.

"Hi Nathan," Marc said.

"Marc! Where have you been?" Nathan asked. "I was looking for⁶ you."

Marc turned to Laura and said, "Hi Laura. This is my friend, Nathan."

1 CU 見到你（See you）
2 foyer [ˈfɔɪɚ] (n.) 劇場休息室；大廳
3 reply [rɪˋplaɪ] (n.) 回覆
4 familiar [fəˋmɪljɚ] (a.) 熟悉的
5 jealous [ˋdʒɛləs] (a.) 妒忌的
6 look for 尋找

"The famous Nathan," Laura laughed, forgetting about Lucy for a moment. "You told Marc he had to come to the auditions."

"*You're* the famous one," Marc said to Laura.

"Famous?" Nathan said, suddenly interested in Laura.

"Her mother's a famous film star," Marc said.

Laura blushed[1] and looked at Lucy.

"I told them about my mother in the audition," Laura said.

Lucy nodded her head slowly and said, "I see."

Laura wanted to change the subject[2]. She introduced Lucy to Marc.

"Marc? This is Lucy, my best friend," Laura said. "I didn't know she was coming to the auditions."

"Sur-prise!" Lucy said, trying to be funny.

"Lucy is an amazing actor," Nathan said.

"Do you live in Pinewood, too?" Marc asked Lucy.

But before Lucy could answer, Laura said they had to go.

"If we don't leave now, we'll miss the train," she said nervously.

She said goodbye, grabbed[3] Lucy's hand, and the two girls walked out of the theater.

"What did I say?" Marc asked.

Nathan shrugged[4]. "I don't know," he said.

Meeting new friends

- Lucy, Laura, Marc and Nathan all meet for the first time. Who introduces who? What do they say?
- In groups of four practice introducing your friends to each other.

---

1 blush [blʌʃ] (v.) 臉紅
2 subject [ˈsʌbdʒɪkt] (n.) 話題
3 grab [græb] (v.) 抓住
4 shrug [ʃrʌg] (v.) (n.) 聳肩
5 stare [stɛr] (v.) 凝視

6 Lucy

 Lucy sat on the train, staring[5] out of the window. Laura was in the toilet, changing back into her normal weekend clothes and taking off her make-up. Lucy couldn't stop thinking about Nathan. Did he really say she was an amazing actor? He was amazing, too, she thought. She smiled as she remembered how Nathan introduced himself to everyone. "Hi. My name's Nathan. I'm just a normal person. I live a normal life in London with my dad. I'm here because I love the theater and I want to be an actor."

Laura came back and sat down opposite[6] Lucy. For a while, the two friends stared at each other without speaking. Then Laura said, "I still can't believe it, Lucy. Why did you go to the auditions? I told my parents I was with you."

"I have dreams, too," Lucy answered.

"No, you don't," Laura said.

"How do you know?" Lucy asked.

"Because I know you," Laura said. "You're my best friend. I know you better than you know yourself."

"No, you don't," Lucy said angrily. "You don't know anything about me. The only thing you know about is yourself. The only thing you ever talk about is yourself. Everything is always about you, you, and more you."

Lucy looked out of the window again. For a moment she thought she saw Nathan's reflection[7] in the glass. Then he disappeared. Lucy looked back at Laura.

6 opposite [ˈɑpəzɪt] (prep.) 在對面   7 reflection [rɪˈflɛkʃən] (n.) 映象

"What exactly did you tell them about your mother?" Lucy asked.

"Nothing," Laura said. "I just told them that she was famous."

"What else did you tell them?"

"I said we lived in Pinewood," Laura said.

"Where's Pinewood?" Lucy asked.

"I don't know," Laura said. "It's the place where the film studios are. They make all the James Bond films there." She paused. "And I think I said my dad was dead."

"Oh, Laura," Lucy said. She sounded disappointed[1] in her friend.

A few minutes later the train arrived at Hitchin station and the two girls got off. They walked along the main road together until Laura turned right to go home.

"See you," said Laura.

"See you," said Lucy.

Lucy watched her friend walk down the street. Why did Laura lie about her mother? Why did she say her father was dead? And why did she lie about where she lived? Was Laura really so unhappy with her real life? Laura didn't know how lucky she was, Lucy thought. Laura's life was a thousand times[2] better than hers. Lucy started walking home. She hoped her parents weren't arguing again.

---

1 disappointed [ˌdɪsəˈpɔɪntɪd] (a.) 失望的
2 time [taɪm] (n.) 倍數

It was two o'clock in the morning and Marc was asleep when his mobile phone[1] rang.[2] He was in the middle of a dream. In his dream, he was walking down a street where everything was made of paper. The buildings were made of paper. The cars were made of paper. Even the people were made of paper. Marc looked down at his hands and they were made of paper too. Then a paper phone rang and Marc woke up. He reached for[3] his phone.

"Hello?" Marc looked to see who was calling, but he couldn't read the name without his glasses. "Who is it?"

"I can't sleep," Nathan said on the phone.

"Why have you woken me up? To tell me you can't sleep?" Marc said.

"No. I want you to tell me about Laura," Nathan said.

"What about her?"

"I don't know. What's she like?"

"Laura?" Marc said, thinking about the girl in the queue outside the theater, the girl talking about her famous mother, the girl running out of the theater with Lucy. "I don't know. I think she's a bit...odd[4]."

"Odd?" Nathan said. "I like her. I can't stop thinking about her." Marc laughed.

"It's because of her famous mother, isn't it?" Marc said.

"No, it's not that," Nathan lied. "Well, maybe, just a little."

"You've found a soulmate[5]." Marc said.

"What do you mean?" Nathan asked.

"Someone who's in the same situation as you."

"You won't tell them, will you?" Nathan said. "Marc? Are you there? It's our secret, right? Promise?"

"I promise," Marc said. "Go to sleep, Nathan."

1 mobile phone [`mobl fon] 手機
2 ring [rɪŋ] (v.) 響（鈴）（動詞三態：ring, rang, rung）
3 reach for 伸手去拿……
4 odd [ɑd] (a.) 怪怪的
5 soulmate [`solmet] (n.) 靈魂伴侶

Three weeks later, Nathan was making breakfast in the kitchen of his London home.

"Dad!" he shouted. "Breakfast's ready!"

Nathan's dad wasn't very good with food. He could eat it but he couldn't make it. Jacquie usually cooked lunch and dinner but Nathan always made breakfast. Jacquie was his dad's number one fan[1]. She was always saying, "I'm your number one fan."

"Good morning, Nathan," Dad said as he walked into the kitchen. "That smells good."

"Hi, Dad," Nathan said. "Fried eggs on toast. Your favorite."

"Why aren't you at school?" Dad asked.

"It's Saturday, Dad."

"Saturday? Oh yes." Nathan's dad sat down at the table and started opening the small pile[2] of letters. "Have you been in the Net yet?" he asked.

"It's on the Net, Dad. You go on the Net[3]."

"Then why is it called Internet[4] and not Onternet?"

"Very funny, Dad," Nathan said. "I printed out[5] your emails. They're on your desk."

"Why can't people leave me alone?" Nathan's dad asked, opening one of the letters.

"Because they love you, Dad," Nathan said, sitting down at the table to eat breakfast.

"This letter's for you," Dad said, looking at the next envelope he picked up. "It's from 'The Green Room'."

Nathan's dad held out the envelope but Nathan didn't take it.
"You open it, Dad," Nathan said. "I'm too nervous."

Nathan's dad opened the envelope and took out the letter inside. He started reading it and his expression⁶ changed. Dad looked serious.

"Well?" Nathan asked. "What does it say?"

1 fan [fæn] (n.) 粉絲;迷
2 pile [paɪl] (n.) (一) 堆
3 the Net 電腦網際網路
   (= the Internet)
4 Internet [ˋɪntəˏnɛt] (n.) 〔電腦〕網際網路
5 print out 將電腦中的檔案列印出來
6 expression [ɪkˋsprɛʃən] (n.) 表情

33

"It's bad news, I'm afraid," Dad said.

"Oh," Nathan said, feeling disappointed.

"I'm sorry, Nathan. You have to spend the summer in London. You've been accepted on the theater course[1]! You did it, Nathan!"

"Dad!" Nathan shouted not knowing what to believe.

Nathan took the letter and started reading. Dad was right. Nathan had passed his audition and had a place at "The Green Room" summer theater school.

Fifty-five miles away in Hitchin, Laura ran to the front door to pick up the post as it fell through the letterbox. Every morning she did the same thing, waiting for the letter to arrive from "The Green Room". She didn't want her parents to see it. They didn't know about her trip to London. She was sure they didn't want her to go on the summer course.

Today the letter finally arrived. She picked it up off the floor, put it in her pocket, and ran upstairs to her room. As she was opening the envelope, her phone started to ring. It was Lucy.

"Hi, Laura. Have you got the letter?" she asked.

"I'm opening it now. And you?"

"Me too," Lucy said.

Laura took the letter from the envelope and started reading quickly.

---

1 course [kors] (n.) 課程
2 application [ˌæpləˈkeʃən] (n.) 申請
3 schedule [ˈskɛdʒʊl] (n.) 課程表
4 website [ˈwɛbˌsaɪt] (n.) 〔電腦〕網站
5 accommodation [əˌkɑməˈdeʃən] (n.) 住宿
6 in order to 為了⋯⋯
7 take part in 參加⋯⋯
8 consent [kənˈsɛnt] (n.) 同意
9 rehearsal [rɪˈhɜsl] (n.) 排練
10 look forward to 期待（後接 名詞或動名詞）
11 associate director 副總監

"The Green Room"
Bedford Square
London

Wednesday, 2 May

Dear Laura,

Many thanks for coming to London to audition for "The Green Room" summer theater school. I am very pleased to inform you that your application[2] to join us has been accepted. Congratulations.

You will find more information about the summer schedule[3] on our website[4] as well as information about accommodation[5] in London, if you need it.

In order to[6] take part in[7] "The Green Room", you must bring a letter from your parents, giving their consent[8]. Bring the letter with you when you come on the first day of rehearsals[9].

We all look forward to[10] seeing you in London in the summer.

Best wishes,

Bob Harrington

Associate Director[11]

"What does your letter say?" Lucy asked.

"It's a YES! I'm going to London!" Laura said, trying to be quiet so that her parents didn't hear.

"Me too!" Lucy shouted down the phone.

"I'm going to be late for work," Marc's Mum said, looking at the envelope on the kitchen table. "Aren't you going to open it?"

"What's the point?" Marc said. "I know what it's going to say. I'm not an actor."

It was true. Marc wasn't an actor. He didn't want to be an actor. It was Nathan who wanted to be an actor. Marc went to the audition because Nathan asked him to go. He remembered his conversation with Nathan.

"I don't know how to act," Marc said.

"Of course you do," Nathan laughed. "Everyone acts all the time."

"I don't," Marc said.

"Don't you ever tell lies?" Nathan asked. "That's the same as acting."

"No, I don't lie," Marc said.

"I don't believe you. You're lying!" Nathan laughed.

"It doesn't matter[1] if you can't act," Mum said. "You're an artist, a very talented[2] artist."

"Thanks, Mum."

Marc's mum looked at herself in the mirror.

"How do I look?" she asked.

Marc looked at his mum in her smart³ black and white police uniform.

"Dangerous," Marc said with a big smile.

His mum kissed him on the cheek and left to go to work. After he heard the front door close, Marc carefully opened the letter.

Dear Marc,

Many thanks for coming to London to audition for "The Green Room" summer theater school. I am sorry to inform you that your application to join us as an actor has not been accepted. I hope you're not too disappointed. However, we were extremely⁴ impressed⁵ with your drawings and would like to offer⁶ you a place on our technical⁷ team to help design⁸ the scenery⁹ and costumes¹⁰ for the summer production. I hope you will accept this offer.

---

1 it doesn't matter 不要緊	6 offer [ˈɔfɚ] (v.) 提供
2 talented [ˈtæləntɪd] (a.) 有才華的	7 technical [ˈtɛknɪkl] (a.) 技術的
3 smart [smɑrt] (a.) 帥氣的	8 design [dɪˈzaɪn] (v.) 設計
4 extremely [ɪkˈstrimlɪ] (adv.) 極度的	9 scenery [ˈsinərɪ] (n.) 舞臺布景
5 impressed [ɪmˈprɛst] (a.) 深刻影響的	10 costume [ˈkɑstjum] (n.) 戲服

Marc couldn't believe his eyes. He read the letter again. They were asking him to go to London.

"Yes!" he shouted.

Letters

- What letter have the four friends received?
- What does this mean for them?
- What will they all do this summer?
- Have you ever received an important letter in the post?

It was the first day of rehearsals and Laura and Lucy were on the train to London.

"What did you tell your parents?" Lucy asked.

"I told them the school was organizing[1] a swimming competition[2] with other schools around the country," Laura said. "I told them I had to practice every day and travel to different places."

"And they believed you?" Lucy said.

"Of course they did," Laura said. "I'm an actor."

"What about the letter?" Lucy asked. "The letter we have to take from our parents?"

Laura smiled and produced an envelope from her sports bag.

"Mum wrote a letter giving her consent for me to take part in the swimming competition," she said. "I copied it last night and changed the swimming competition to the theater school. It's a good forgery[3]."

"I don't understand why you don't tell your parents the truth," Lucy said.

---

1 organize [ˈɔrgəˌnaɪz] (v.) 組織
2 competition [ˌkɑmpəˈtɪʃən] (n.) 競賽
3 forgery [ˈfɔrdʒərɪ] (n.) 偽造之物

"Because they won't understand," Laura said. "They only understand their own boring[1] lives and they want me to live the same boring life. I want to be different. I want to be special. Did *you* tell *your* parents?"

Lucy looked out the window. "Yeah. But they don't care what I do," she said. "They're happy I'm going to be out of the house all summer. They'll have more time to fight and argue with each other."

"Sometimes I wish my parents argued more often," Laura said.

"Don't say that," Lucy said. "Don't ever say that. I like your mum and dad. They seem really happy together. You should tell them the truth. One day your lies are going to get you into trouble."

Lies

- List all the things Laura lies about. What do you think of Laura's lies?
- Do you sometimes lie in this way? Why?

Laura looked at her friend with a serious expression.

"You won't say anything, will you?" she said. "If anyone asks, I live with my famous mother in Pinewood. And my father is dead."

"Do you think people will really think you're more special if you have an imaginary[2] famous mother?" Lucy said. "What's her name anyway? Jones—like you?"

"She changed her name when she became famous," Laura said. "And don't forget that you live in Pinewood, too."

"No," Lucy said. "I'm not going to lie about my life. You can live in Pinewood if you want but I live in Hitchin."

"But you're my best friend. It will look suspicious[3] if we live in different places."

"No," Lucy said. "NO."

They were arriving in London. Lucy looked out the window at the houses passing by[4].

"I wonder where Nathan lives?" she thought to herself.

1 boring [ˈbɔrɪŋ] (a.) 無聊的
2 imaginary [ɪˈmædʒəˌnɛrɪ] (a.) 虛構的
3 suspicious [səˈspɪʃəs] (a.) 可疑的
4 pass by 經過

When Nathan and Marc arrived at the theater, they went through to the auditorium. There were about thirty teenagers there. Nathan and Marc recognized[1] some of the people from the audition but other faces were new.

"Where is she?" Nathan asked, looking around. "Where's Laura?"

"Maybe she didn't pass the audition," Marc said. He took out his notebook and started to draw a picture of Nathan, standing on the stage, holding a broken heart. Then he drew big broken heart and wrote "N loves L" beside it.

"I don't *love* her," Nathan said, looking at the picture.

"No?" Marc said. "You haven't stopped talking about her since the auditions."

"There's something different about her," Nathan said. "She's… different."

"You're different, too, remember?" Marc said. "You'll have to tell her one day."

"Tell her what?" Nathan asked.

"About your dad," Marc said.

"That's our secret," Nathan said angrily. "Don't tell anyone. You promised."

Laura and Lucy walked into the auditorium and Nathan's face suddenly lit up. He waved to them and the two girls came and sat down next to the boys. They all smiled and laughed and talked about the letters they received. Then Lucy saw Marc's notebook and the drawing of Nathan.

recognize [ˈrɛkəɡˌnaɪz] (v.) 認出

"What are you drawing?" Lucy asked Marc.

"Nothing," Marc said, closing his notebook quickly.

But it was too late. Lucy saw Nathan's broken heart with "N loves L" written beside it. "Nathan loves Lucy," she thought.

Then Bob, the young man with red hair from the auditions, appeared on the stage and welcomed the students to "The Green Room".

"Today you're all going to set off[1] on a journey[2]," he said. "It's not going to be an easy journey and we will probably lose some of you on the way. But if you are prepared to work hard and work together then this will be a journey you will remember for the rest of your lives. Are you ready to start?"

Everyone in the auditorium shouted back, "Yes!"

"I can't hear you!" Bob shouted.

"Yes!!" everyone shouted again.

Journey

- What is the journey Bob is talking about?
- Have you ever been on a similar journey?
- Think of another word to describe this "journey".

[1] set off 動身
[2] journey [ˈdʒɜˈnɪ] (n.) 旅程

11 Bob

   Bob enjoyed shouting. The first few days at "The Green
Room" summer theater school were like being at a military[1]
school. The days started at 9 o'clock with a physical[2] warm-up[3]
session[4]. First, everyone had to stand and shake their bodies to
wake themselves up. Then Bob shouted orders for everyone to
do press-ups[5] and sit-ups[6]. Then there were breathing and voice
exercises. Bob liked doing these because he could shout orders
and make strange sounds at the same time. Everyone had to
move their mouths into strange shapes and imitate[7] the noises
that Bob made. Then everyone shouted and sang and made
more strange noises until Bob shouted, "Stop!"

After the warm-up session, there were drama[8] classes. For the
drama classes, the students were divided[9] into three groups.
Bob took one group and two other teachers took the others. In
the first week they did a lot of "trust[10] exercises". Bob said it was
very important for actors to trust each other. Bob's favorite trust
exercise was called "The Chickie[11] Run".

"OK, everybody," Bob said. "We need a lot of space for this."

Everyone moved the chairs to the side of the room. It was a
long room with mirrors on both sides. The mirrors made the
room look even bigger. First, he told everyone to stand against
one of the end walls. Then he asked for a volunteer[12]. Nathan
stepped forward[13].

"Very good, Nathan," Bob said. "I want you to go to the other end of the room."

Nathan walked to the end of the long room and looked back at everyone standing along the opposite wall.

1 military [ˈmɪləˌtɛrɪ] (a.) 軍事的
2 physical [ˈfɪzɪkl̩] (a.) 身體的
3 warm-up [ˈwɔrmˌʌp] (n.) 暖身運動
4 session [ˈsɛʃən] (n.)（授課活動的）時間
5 press-up [ˈprɛsˌʌp] (n.) 伏地挺身
6 sit-up [ˈsɪtˌʌp] (n.) 仰臥起坐
7 imitate [ˈɪməˌtet] (v.) 模仿
8 drama [ˈdrɑmə] (n.) 戲劇
9 divide [dəˈvaɪd] (v.) 分開
10 trust [trʌst] (n.) 信任
11 chickie [ˈtʃɪkɪ] (n.) 小雞
12 volunteer [ˌvɑlənˈtɪr] (n.) 志願者
13 forward [ˈfɔrwɚd] (adv.) 向前

"Now, listen carefully, Nathan," Bob said. "I want you to close your eyes and run as fast as you can towards[1] the wall at the other end of the room. Nothing will happen to you. We're going to catch you before you hit the wall." He looked at the others. "Isn't that right? We're going to catch Nathan." He looked back at Nathan. "All you have to do, Nathan, is keep your eyes closed, run as fast as you can, and trust everyone. Can you do that?"

Nathan wasn't sure if he trusted everyone but he knew he had to do it. So he breathed in, closed his eyes, and started running. It felt strange to be running with his eyes closed. At first he thought he would hit something or someone. But then for a few seconds he felt free before he felt the arms of the others catching him.

Bob told them that he called the exercise "The Chickie Run" because of a scene from an old film called *Rebel*[2] *Without a Cause*.

In the film, two teenagers drive their cars towards the edge[3] of a cliff[4] and have to jump out before the cars go over the cliff. One of them jumps out but the other one doesn't.

"The film starred[5] James Dean," Bob said. "He was a method actor. Does anyone know what method[6] acting is?"

James Dean

Nathan raised his hand.

"It's an acting technique[7]," Nathan said. "The actor *becomes* the character[8] they are playing."

"That's right," Bob said. "You don't just read the lines[9] in the script[10]. You become the person who is speaking those lines. You think like that person. You behave[11] like that person."

A girl at the back of the room laughed.

"What happens if your character is a killer[12]?" she asked. "Do you have to kill people?"

"Of course not," Bob said. "But you have to get inside the mind of the killer. You have to find out[13] why that person became a killer. What happened in his or her life? Sometimes it can be a frightening[14] experience. That's why you have to trust each other."

Acting

- What do actors have to do when they act?
- Who do they have to trust?
- Have you ever done any acting?

---

1 towards [tə`wɔrdz] (prep.) 朝向
2 rebel [`rɛbl] (n.) 反抗者
3 edge [ɛdʒ] (n.) 邊緣
4 cliff [klɪf] (n.) 懸崖
5 star [stɑr] (v.) 擔任主角
6 method [`mɛθəd] (n.) 方法
7 technique [tɛk`nik] (n.) 技術

8 character [`kærɪktə] (n.) 角色
9 lines [laɪnz] (n.) 〔複〕台詞
10 script [skrɪpt] (n.) 劇本
11 behave [bɪ`hev] (v.) 表現
12 killer [`kɪlə] (n.) 殺手
13 find out 找出來（真相、原因等）
14 frightening [`fraɪtnɪŋ] (a.) 令人驚嚇的

In the afternoons, all the students worked on the show they were going to put on[1]. Marc went with the technical team to design the sets[2] and costumes while the others rehearsed. This year's Green Room production was called *What You Will*[3]. Dame Helen told everyone about it on the first afternoon.

"*What You Will* is the alternative[4] title of William Shakespeare's play *Twelfth Night*," she said. "And we are going to produce an alternative version[5] of his play. We are going to start with Shakespeare's story and characters and we are going to add[6] our own words, music and dance."

Dame Helen also said that tomorrow was the day for casting[7] the play. She told them that casting was another important part of being an actor. When directors *cast* a play or a film, they look for the right actors for the different characters or parts[8].

Nathan knew that if he wanted a good part in the show, he needed to do some homework. When he got home that evening, he went to his room and downloaded Shakespeare's original[9] version of *Twelfth Night*. Then he did some research[10]. He discovered[11] that Shakespeare wrote the play around 1601.

1 put on 演出
2 set [sɛt] (n.) 場景
3 what you will 隨心所欲
　(= what you want)
4 alternative [ɔlˋtɝnətɪv] (a.) 兩選一的
5 version [ˋvɝʒən] (n.) 版本
6 add [æd] (v.) 添加
7 cast [kæst] (v.) 選角色

8 part [pɑrt] (n.) 角色
9 original [əˋrɪdʒənl] (a.) 原著的
10 research [rɪˋsɝtʃ] (n.) 研究
11 discover [dɪsˋkʌvɚ] (v.) 發現
12 comedy [ˋkɑmədɪ] (n.) 喜劇
13 identity [aɪˋdɛntətɪ] (n.) 身分
14 extract [ˋɛkstrækt] (n.) 片段
15 verse [vɝs] (n.) 詩；韻文

The play is a comedy[12] about mistaken identities[13] and starts with one of Shakespeare's most famous lines—"If music be the food of love, play on". These first words are spoken by a character called Orsino. When Nathan started reading the script, he knew immediately that he wanted to play the part of Orsino.

The next afternoon, Dame Helen and Bob asked the students to read extracts[14] from Shakespeare's play.

Some of the students found it difficult to read Shakespeare's English. People spoke differently in the 1600s. A lot of the words seem old today and Shakespeare wrote in verse[15].

Lucy was good, Nathan thought. And Laura was better. Then it was time for Nathan to speak.

"If music be the food of love, play on," he said. "Give me excess[1] of it, that, surfeiting[2], the appetite[3] may sicken[4], and so die." Nathan knew the whole speech by heart[5] and everyone applauded when he reached the end.

"I think we've found our Orsino," Dame Helen said.

The next morning, the cast list[6] was stuck[7] to the noticeboard[8]. Nathan had the part of Orsino, Laura had the part of Viola, and Lucy had the part of Olivia. The three friends had the three most important parts in the play.

---

1 excess [ɪkˈsɛs] (n.) 過量
2 surfeit [ˈsɝfɪt] (v.) 過飽
3 appetite [ˈæpəˌtaɪt] (n.) 胃口
4 sicken [ˈsɪkən] (v.) 使作嘔
5 by heart 默背下來
6 cast list 卡司名單
7 stick [stɪk] (v.) 黏貼（動詞三態：stick, stuck, stuck）
8 noticeboard [ˈnotɪsˌbɔrd] (n.) 布告欄
9 How's it going?〔問候語〕可好？
10 liar [ˈlaɪɚ] (n.) 說謊的人

13 Lucy, Marc

On the fourth day, Lucy was going to rehearsals when she saw Marc in the coffee shop next to the theater. She went inside and sat down opposite him. Marc was busy drawing in his notebook.

"Hi Marc," Lucy said. "How's it going⁹?"

Marc looked up and smiled when he saw Lucy.

"Hi, Lucy," he said. "How are you?"

"Not bad," she said. She looked out the window for a moment and then said, "Tell me about Nathan."

Marc was surprised by the question.

"What do you want to know?" he asked.

"I don't know," she said. "He never talks about himself. Where does he live? What do his parents do? How did you meet him?"

Marc didn't know what to say. He couldn't tell Lucy the truth.

He had promised Nathan, he couldn't say anything about his dad or his life in London. But Marc was not a good liar¹⁰. So he told Lucy the truth.

"I'm sorry, Lucy," he said. "I can't tell you."

"Why not?" Lucy asked. "Is it a secret?"

Marc blushed.

"It is a secret," Lucy said. Then she laughed.

"What's funny?" Marc asked.

"You can't tell me about Nathan because it's a secret and I can't tell you about Laura because it's a secret," she said.

Marc looked at Lucy. He wanted to ask about Laura's secret but he knew Lucy couldn't tell him. And he couldn't tell her Nathan's secret.

"Why do you want to know about Nathan?" he asked.

"It's a secret," Lucy said, laughing again. "What are you drawing?"

"It's an idea for the set," Marc said. "I'm still working on it."

"Can I see?"

Marc gave the notebook to Lucy and she looked at the drawing.

"It's good," she said. "I like it."

"Really?"

Lucy started turning the pages of the notebook and stopped when she saw the picture of Nathan standing on the stage with the broken heart. Marc could see her looking at the writing beside the drawing—"N loves L".

"Oh, no," he thought. "Does she think L is for Lucy?"

"Thanks," Lucy said, closing the book and giving it back to Marc.

Marc didn't know what to say. He didn't want to hurt Lucy's feelings and tell her the truth. So he didn't say anything. He was sure that Lucy could see the expression on his face and realize that L wasn't for Lucy. L was for Laura. But sometimes people don't see what they should see. They only see what they want to see.

"Nathan's lucky," she said, "having you as a friend. Tell me about *your* life. Or is that a secret too?"

"There's not a lot to tell," Marc said. "I live in South London with my mum. She's a police officer[1]. My dad lives in Manchester so I don't see him much. They divorced[2]. Then he re-married[3]. So now he has another family. What about you? Do you have any brothers or sisters?"

But Lucy wasn't listening. She was thinking about Nathan.

Secrets

- What are some of the secrets in the story?
- Who secretly likes who?
- Do you secretly like anyone?

1 police officer 警察
2 divorce [dəˋvors] (v.) 離婚
3 re-marry [riˋmærɪ] (v.) 再婚
4 go out 熄滅
5 spotlight [ˋspɑk͵laɪt] (n.) 聚光燈
6 silence [ˋsaɪləns] (n.) 寂靜
7 for a moment 一會兒
8 sink [sɪŋk] (v.) 下沉 (動詞三態：
   sink; sank/sunk; sunk/sunken)
9 drown [draʊn] (v.) 溺斃
10 scared [skɛrd] (a.) 嚇壞的
11 dress as 打扮成⋯⋯
12 duke [djuk] (n.) 公爵

On the first afternoon of the second week, Bob asked all the actors to meet him on the stage of the theater. This was their first time on the stage and they were all excited. They looked up at the lights above them and then out at all the empty seats in the auditorium. There was one person sitting in the middle of the auditorium. It was Bob.

"Lights!" Bob shouted.

All the lights in the theater suddenly went out[4] apart from one spotlight[5] at the front of the stage. Everyone stopped talking and there was silence[6] for a moment[7].

"I want you to think back to your auditions," Bob said. "At your auditions, we asked you to stand up and introduce yourselves. Remember? Well, now I want you to take it in turns to stand in the spotlight and introduce your character to the audience in your own words. I want to know who you are in the show and how you feel. OK? When you're ready..."

Nobody moved for a moment. Then Laura walked to the front of the stage and stood in the spotlight.

"My name is Viola," she said. "I was in an accident. I don't remember much about it. I was in a ship with my twin brother, Sebastian, and the ship sank[8]. I don't know what happened to Sebastian. He probably drowned[9]. After the accident, I was scared[10] to be alone as a woman so I dressed as[11] a man and called myself Cesario. Then I met the Duke[12]."

Laura looked at Nathan who walked into the spotlight.

"Hi. I'm the Duke," he said. "Duke Orsino of Illyria[1]. I'm also a poet[2]. When I first saw Cesario, I thought he looked honest. So I gave him a job. You see, I'm in love with Olivia who lives near here. She says she doesn't love me but I don't believe her. Anyway, she refuses[3] to speak to me so I've asked Cesario to speak to her and put in a good word[4] for me."

Lucy walked into the spotlight.

"He's talking about me. I'm Olivia. My brother died recently and I don't have time for the Duke. He's self-centered[5] and stupid. I don't feel anything for him. So when he sends[6] this young man, Cesario, to see me, my first reaction[7] is to tell him to get lost[8]. But Cesario is very good-looking. I think I am falling in love with[9] Cesario, but not with the Duke."

"Very good!" Bob shouted from the auditorium.

1 Illyria [ɪ'lɪrɪə] (n.) 伊利亞
2 poet ['poɪt] (n.) 詩人
3 refuse [rɪ'fjuz] (v.) 不肯
4 put in a good word 説好話
5 self-centered [,sɛlf'sɛntəd] (a.) 自我中心的
6 send [sɛnd] (v.) 派遣（動詞三態：send; sent; sent）
7 reaction [rɪ'ækʃən] (n.) 反應
8 get lost 走開（= go away）
9 fall in love with somebody 愛上某人
10 illusion [ɪ'ljuʒən] (n.) 錯覺
11 deception [dɪ'sɛpʃən] (n.) 欺騙
12 pretend [prɪ'tɛnd] (v.) 假裝
13 title ['taɪtl̩] (n.) 標題
14 mad [mæd] (a.) 瘋狂的
15 imitate ['ɪmə,tet] (v.) 模仿
16 surly ['sɝlɪ] (a.) 無禮的；態度惡劣的
17 google ['gugl̩] (v.) 上網搜尋

All the other actors introduced themselves and helped to tell the story of *What You Will*. When they reached the end of the story, Bob came onto the stage and told everyone to sit down.

"So what is our show about?" he asked the actors.

"Illusion[10]", said Lucy. "I fall in love with Cesario and I don't realize that he's a woman."

"Deception[11]," Laura said. "I'm pretending[12] to be a man when I'm really a woman."

"Love," Nathan said. "I'm in love with Olivia, who is in love with Cesario, who is in love with me!"

"You're all right," Bob said. "It's about the mad things we think, see and do when we are in love. Even the title[13] of the play is mad[14]. *What You Will* means 'whatever you want'. In fact, if Shakespeare were alive today, he'd probably call it *Whatever*."

The actors laughed as Bob imitated[15] a surly[16] teenager shrugging his shoulders and saying the word that parents hate most—*whatever*.

Whatever

- Can you think of a word in your language that is similar to "whatever"?

At the end of rehearsals, Nathan went to speak to Laura.

"I *googled*[17] you last night," he said.

"You did *what*?" Laura said.

"I searched for you on the Internet," Nathan said. "Do you know how many Laura Joneses there are in the world?" Laura didn't reply. "Anyway, I didn't find you or your famous mother."

"She changed her name," Laura said, walking away.

When Nathan told Marc about his search for Laura on the Internet, Marc told him that she had a secret.

"How do you know?" Nathan asked.

"Lucy told me," he said. Marc didn't tell Nathan about the other things that Lucy said.

"Let's follow them to Pinewood on Monday," Nathan said. "Maybe we can find out what Laura's secret is and who her famous mother is."

Marc didn't think this was a good idea.

"That's spying[1]," Marc said. "I don't think we should."

But Marc always did what Nathan told him to do.

On Tuesday afternoon, after rehearsals, the two friends followed Laura and Lucy from the theater to King's Cross station.

Nathan and Marc often saw people following other people in spy films and TV series but it was more difficult in real life. They nearly lost the girls as they crossed Euston Road and disappeared into King's Cross Station. Inside, the station was busy. Nathan and Marc looked around but they couldn't see Laura and Lucy. Then they saw them in the distance[2], walking towards platform[3] 2.

"We need tickets," Marc said.

They went to the ticket office and asked for two return tickets to Pinewood. The woman in the ticket office laughed.

"Pinewood isn't a place," she said. "If you want to go to Pinewood Film Studios, you need to go to Denham. Trains to Denham leave from Marylebone Station."

"Where is the train on platform 2 going?" Nathan asked.

"Peterborough," she said.

"Then we'll have two return tickets to Peterborough, please," he said. They walked quickly to platform 2 and got on the train to Peterborough. They could see Laura and Lucy sitting at the end of the carriage⁴.

"Have they seen us?" Nathan asked as the train left the station.

"I don't think so," Marc replied.

Half an hour later they saw Laura and Lucy get off the train. They followed them out of Hitchin station and down the main road to the corner where Laura turned right.

"Now what do we do?" Marc asked, watching Lucy and Laura go in different directions.

"You follow Lucy and I'll follow Laura," Nathan said. "We'll meet at the station in twenty minutes."

---

1 spy [spaɪ] (v.) 監視 (n.) 密探   3 platform [ˈplætˌfɔrm] (n.) 月臺
2 distance [ˈdɪstəns] (n.) 遠處   4 carriage [ˈkærɪdʒ] (n.) 鐵路客車廂

One minute later Nathan watched as Laura opened the front door to her house and walked inside.

"Mum? Dad? I'm home!" she shouted as she closed the front door behind her.

Nathan stood on the pavement[1] looking at the house. It was an ordinary[2] semi-[3]detached[4] two-storey[5] house with a small front garden and a garage with a car parked outside. "It doesn't look like a film star's[6] house," he thought. "And we're not in Pinewood. And her dad isn't dead."

At the same time, Marc was following Lucy down a narrow road. There were trees on either side of the road and several large detached houses. Lucy stopped outside one of the houses. She looked up at the house and Marc thought she was going to go inside. But Lucy changed her mind and continued walking down the road. Marc walked to the house and looked up at the windows. He could see and hear a man and woman arguing inside. "They must be Lucy's parents," Marc thought. He stared at the house for a while and then turned and walked back in the direction of the station.

"I told you this was a bad idea," Marc said when he saw Nathan.

"Let's go home," Nathan said.

The two boys didn't say anything all the way back to London.

The truth

- What do Marc and Nathan find out about Lucy and Laura?
- Do they like what they find out?
- Do you think following people is a good idea? Discuss with a partner.

16 Laura, Lucy

At rehearsals the next day, Bob asked the actors to read through the final act[7] of the play.

During the play, Viola (Laura) falls in love with the Duke (Nathan). Meanwhile, Viola's twin brother, Sebastian, arrives. He didn't drown in the accident. Olivia (Lucy) thinks Sebastian is Cesario (Viola dressed as a man) and asks him to marry her. When the Duke discovers that Cesario is not a man but really a woman (Viola), he realizes that he is in love with her.

"Stop!" Bob shouted before they reached the end. "This is a comedy, not a tragedy[8]."

Bob was looking at Nathan who was acting strangely today. He was forgetting his lines and he looked unhappy. When his character had to tell Viola that he loved her, he spoke the words without any emotion[9].

"What's wrong with you, Nathan?" Bob asked. "Has someone died?"

Nathan looked at the floor. He was thinking about yesterday and he couldn't concentrate[10] on his acting.

"It's a stupid play," Nathan eventually[11] said.

"Of course it's stupid," Bob said. "It's a comedy."

Everyone laughed except Nathan.

---

1 pavement [ˈpevmənt] (n.) 人行道
2 ordinary [ˈɔrdn̩ˌɛrɪ] (a.) 普通的
3 semi- [ˈsɛmɪ] (pref.) 半的
4 detached [dɪˈtætʃt] (a.) 不連接的
5 storey [ˈstɔrɪ] (n.) 樓層
6 film star 電影明星
7 final act 最後一場戲
8 tragedy [ˈtrædʒədɪ] (n.) 悲劇
9 emotion [ɪˈmoʃən] (n.) 情感
10 concentrate [ˈkɑnsɛnˌtret] (v.) 集中精神
11 eventually [ɪˈvɛntʃʊəlɪ] (n.) 終於地

"I don't understand why I fall in love with her," Nathan said, without looking at Laura. "She lied to me. She pretended to be a boy."

"I don't know why I love *you* either," Laura laughed. "You're moody[1] and self-centered and you were in love with *her* until five minutes ago."

Nathan looked up. Laura was pointing[2] at Lucy.

"At least I didn't pretend to be someone else," Nathan said to Laura.

Bob could sense[3] that something was wrong. He told everyone to take a break[4] and leave the room, apart from Nathan and Laura.

"What's wrong with you two?" Bob asked when they were alone. When neither of them spoke, Bob said, "I'm going to leave you both alone. Talk to each other and sort out[5] the problem. I need to believe that you love each other."

Bob left the room. Laura looked at Nathan. She knew that he was angry about something.

"What's wrong?" she asked.

"I know your secret," Nathan said.

"Are you talking to me or to Viola?" she asked.

"To you," he said. "I'm talking to Laura, if that's your real name."

"Of course it's my real name. What are you going on about[6]?"

"I know your secret," Nathan said again.

"What secret?" she asked nervously.

"You lied. You lied to all of us."

Laura looked away.

"I don't know what you're talking about," she said.

"You don't have a famous mother," Nathan said. "Your father isn't dead. And you don't live in Pinewood. In fact, Pinewood doesn't exist[7]. It's just the name of a film studio."

"How did you find out?" Laura asked. "Was it Lucy? It was Lucy, wasn't it?"

"It's not important how I found out," Nathan said. "Why did you lie?"

Laura suddenly felt embarrassed[8] and angry. She turned and walked out of the rehearsal room.

Lucy was waiting for Laura in the corridor.

"Is everything all right?" Lucy asked.

"How could you do that to me?" Laura said angrily. "I thought you were my friend."

"Do *what*?" Lucy asked, surprised.

"Don't pretend you don't know," Laura said. "And don't ever talk to me again!"

Laura walked down the corridor and disappeared round the corner. Lucy didn't know what to do. Should she follow her friend or talk to Nathan? She walked into the rehearsal room and saw Nathan sitting in the corner with his head in his hands.

"What happened?" Lucy asked. "What's wrong with Laura? Is she jealous?"

---

1 moody [ˈmudɪ] (a.) 陰晴不定的
2 point [pɔɪnt] (v.) 指向
3 sense [sɛns] (v.) 感到
4 take a break 休息一下
5 sort out 解決（問題）
6 What are you going on about? 你在扯什麼？(= What are you talking about?)
7 exist [ɪgˈzɪst] (v.) 存在
8 embarrassed [ɪmˈbærəst] (a.) 尷尬的

"Jealous?" Nathan looked up at Lucy. "What do you mean?"
Lucy sat down next to Nathan.

"Did you tell her about us?" Lucy said.

"Us?" Nathan said, feeling even more confused[1].

"Don't worry," she said. "I feel the same as you."

"How do you know what I feel?" Nathan asked.

"I saw the drawing," she said. "Marc showed it to me."

"Marc? What are you talking about?" Nathan suddenly remembered Marc's drawing of Nathan holding a broken heart with "N loves L" written beside it.

"Oh no," Nathan said. "You think I..."

But before he could finish the sentence, Bob walked into the room, followed by all the other students.

"OK!" Bob shouted. "Listen, everyone! Let's start again from the beginning of the final act. Take your places[2]!"

Nathan didn't have to say anything more. Lucy understood. "How could I be so stupid?" she thought. "L was for Laura—not Lucy!"

Lucy ran out of the rehearsal room, with Nathan calling after her.

"Lucy! Come back!"

---

1 confused [kənˈfjuzd] (a.) 搞糊塗了
2 take your place 就定位

When Marc phoned Nathan that evening, Nathan didn't answer. He didn't want to talk to Marc. "Why did Marc show Lucy the drawing?" Nathan asked himself. "He probably told her my secret, too. Now everyone will know about Dad."

"Dinner's ready!" Jacquie shouted from downstairs.

Nathan didn't talk much at the dinner table that evening. Dad looked at his son as Jacquie took away the pasta[1] bowl and brought the dessert[2]—chocolate brownies[3] with ice-cream.

"My favorite," Dad said when he saw the brownies.

"I know," said Jacquie. "I'm your number one fan, remember? I know everything about you."

"I thought fried eggs on toast was your favorite," Nathan said.

"That's his favorite breakfast," Jacquie said. "Brownies are his favorite dessert. It was in issue[4] 145 of *Greatest Hits*[5] magazine."

Jacquie left the room to make a phone call. Nathan stared at the wall. "It isn't easy being the son of one of the most famous rock[6] musicians in the world," he thought.

Are you famous?

- Why do think being the son of a famous rock star is not easy? Discuss with a partner.

"How's 'The Green Room' going?" Dad asked Nathan. "Have you made any new friends or met anyone special?"

"Why do you ask?" Nathan said.

"Because you look miserable[7]," Dad said. "Come on, Nathan. Talk to me."

Nathan put down his dessert spoon and took a deep breath.

"Don't be angry, Dad," Nathan began. "I think you're amazing, really, I do. But sometimes I feel as if I don't exist."

"Go on," Dad said.

"At school, all the other kids only want to know me because of you. They want to be my friends so they can come home and meet my famous dad. Nobody's interested in me."

"Not everybody," Dad said. "Marc has always been a good friend."

"Exactly," Nathan said. "Marc didn't know who I was when I met him. That's why I liked him. That's why I trusted him."

"Trusted—in the past? What has Marc done? "

"He showed a drawing to a girl and now she thinks I'm in love with her. But I'm not in love with her. It's her friend that...I like...a lot."

"And the friend's name is...?"

"Laura," Nathan said. "She told everyone that she was the daughter of a famous film star. I believed her. I thought we could be real friends because we both have famous parents. But then I discovered it was a lie."

---

1 pasta [ˈpɑstɑ] (n.) 義大利麵
2 dessert [dɪˈzɜt] (n.) 甜點
3 brownie [ˈbraʊnɪ] (n.) 一種巧克力
   蛋糕或餅乾

4 issue [ˈɪʃju] (n.) (報刊) 期號
5 hit [hɪt] (n.) 熱門 (歌曲、電影等)
6 rock [rɑk] (n.) 搖滾樂
7 miserable [ˈmɪzərəbl] (a.) 很不快樂

"Ah!" Dad laughed. "And how does Laura feel about your famous dad?"

"She doesn't know," Nathan said. "When I auditioned for 'The Green Room', I didn't tell anyone who I was or who my dad was. I wanted to get into the school because I'm a good actor. Not because my dad is a famous star. And I did it. I got into the school. Then I met this girl, and now everything's a mess."

"Let me tell you what I think," Dad said. "I think you're hurt. A person you like very much has told a lie. That's the problem. If you like her then it's not important who her parents are. She probably lied because she wanted to be different—to be special. You did the same, pretending to be someone you're not."

"That's different," Nathan said. "I just wanted to be normal."

"You *are* normal, Nathan. Even I am normal, believe it or not. Do you think people are different because they are famous?"

"No."

"There will always be people who will want to know you because of your famous dad or because you're famous. But give people time. You'll soon discover who your real friends are. I'm speaking from experience."

"So what should I do?" Nathan asked.

"You know what to do," Dad said. "But first, you can check my emails."

Advice

- What advice does Nathan's dad give him?
- Do you agree with this advice?
- Imagine you are Nathan, what do you do next?

The next morning, Lucy didn't meet Laura at Hitchin station so Laura took the train to London alone. "Maybe Lucy took an earlier train to avoid seeing me," Laura thought. As she sat on the train, looking out the window, Laura thought she saw Nathan's reflection in the glass. Then he disappeared.

Was it really possible that Nathan liked her? Well, if he did like her, he probably didn't like her anymore. "I wish I hadn't lied," Laura said to herself. She was a good actor. She didn't need to lie. She didn't need a famous mother to be successful or popular. Look at Nathan. He was one of the most popular students at the theater school and he was just a normal person.

As the train arrived in London, Laura looked out the window at the houses passing by. "I wonder where Nathan lives," she thought to herself.

All morning, Laura tried to avoid Nathan. She didn't know what to say to him or how to act. So she stood at the back of the rehearsal room for the morning exercise sessions and pretended not to hear him when he called to her at the end of the class.

"Laura! I need to talk to you!"

She managed to[1] lose[2] him in the crowd of students going to the cafeteria. Then she walked out of the building and waited in the street until the morning break ended. She was going back inside when Marc walked past.

---

[1] manage to 設法
[2] lose [luz] (v.) 擺脫

Friends

- Why are all the four friends avoiding each other?
- Do you ever avoid your friends? Why?

"Hi, Laura," he said. "Have you seen Lucy?"

"No," Laura said. "Why?"

"It's probably nothing," Marc said. "I saw her leaving the theater yesterday and she looked really upset. I tried to talk to her but she ran away. Then I phoned Nathan in the evening but he didn't answer my calls. I haven't seen Lucy today so I thought...Did anything happen yesterday?"

Before Laura could answer, Bob appeared.

"Laura?" he said. "Dame Helen wants to talk to you—*now*."

Laura walked down the corridor to Dame Helen's office. She was nervous. What did Dame Helen want to talk to Laura about? Did Nathan tell her about the lies? Had something happened to Lucy? She knocked on the door and waited.

"Come in!" Dame Helen called.

Laura opened the door and got the shock of her life. Sitting in the room with Dame Helen were her mother and father.

"Mum? Dad? What are you doing here?" she asked.

Before they could answer, Dame Helen told Laura to come in.

"The good news," said Dame Helen with a smile, "is that your father is alive. The bad news is that neither he nor your mother knew you were here." She held up the letter that Laura brought with her on the first day. "I understand that this letter is a forgery."

"Why didn't you tell us?" Laura's dad said. "Why did you lie to us and tell us you were going to swimming practice?"

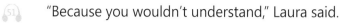

"Because you wouldn't understand," Laura said.

Dame Helen laughed.

"I find that very hard to believe[1]," she said.

"Why? What do you mean?" Laura asked.

"Your mother understands a lot about the theater," Dame Helen said. "Isn't that right, Rose?"

Laura's mum smiled at her daughter.

"I'm sure you'll find this hard to believe," her mum said, "but I wanted to be an actress when I was your age."

Laura couldn't believe it.

Hard to believe

- What does Laura discover about her parents?
- Have you ever discovered anything new about your parents? Tell a partner about it.

"In fact," she continued. "I also studied here at 'The Green Room'. This is where I met Helen...and your father."

"Dad?" Laura said. "You wanted to be an actor, too?"

Laura's dad laughed.

"I wasn't as good as your mother," he said. "She was the one with the real talent[2]."

"Why didn't you tell me?" Laura asked.

"You never talk to us, Laura," her dad said.

"And we never thought you were interested," said her mum. "You spent all your time at swimming practice. Well, that's what we thought."

"Your mother was destined[3] to become a star," Dame Helen said. "But she decided that having a family was more important."

"How did you find out that I was here?" Laura asked. "Did Lucy tell you?"

"Your friend, Lucy, is completely[4] innocent[5]," said Dame Helen. "When I first saw you, I thought your face was familiar. Then, when I saw you act the part of Viola, I knew for sure. That's when I phoned my old friend, Rose."

"So, what's going to happen?" Laura asked. "Do I have to leave the theater school?"

---

1 hard to believe 難以置信
2 talent ['tælənt] (n.) 有天分的人
3 destined ['dɛstɪnd] (a.) 預定的
4 completely [kəm'plitlɪ] (adv.) 完全地
5 innocent ['ɪnəsn̩t] (a.) 清白的

Marc got off the train at Hitchin station and followed the road into town and on to Lucy's house. Marc knew something was wrong. Why did Lucy run away from him yesterday? Why didn't Nathan answer his calls? Why did Dame Helen want to talk to Laura? And why didn't Lucy come to "The Green Room" today?

Marc reached the house but he knew Lucy wasn't inside. He continued along the road, following the steps that Lucy took the other day. There was a park at the end of the road and Marc went inside. There were some tennis courts[1] in the park, some benches[2] and a bandstand. Marc could see someone sitting on the floor of the bandstand[3], listening to an MP3 player. He walked closer and recognized Lucy.

"Hello," Marc said, looking down at Lucy. She didn't hear him at first but she got a shock when she looked up and saw him.

"Marc! What are you doing here?" Lucy asked, switching off[4] the music. "How did you find me?"

Marc sat down beside her.

"My parents fought a lot before they got a divorce," he said. "I had a place like this. A place to go when I didn't want to go home or when they started fighting."

"But how did you know where I live?" Lucy asked.

Marc told Lucy about the other day. He told her how they followed her and Laura to King's Cross station and onto the train to Hitchin. He told her how Nathan followed Laura and how he followed Lucy.

"Why did you follow us?" Lucy asked angrily. "That's creepy[5]."

"It was Nathan's idea," Marc said. "People do stupid things when they're in love."

"I feel such an idiot," Lucy said. "When I saw the drawing in your notebook, I thought L was for Lucy—not Laura!"

1 tennis court 網球場	4 switch off 關掉（開關）
2 bench [bɛntʃ] (n.) 長椅	5 creepy [ˋkripɪ] (a.) 令人發毛的
3 bandstand [ˋbænd͵stænd] (n.) 露天音樂臺	

"I know," Marc said apologetically[1]. "I should've told you. I'm sorry."

"Why didn't you tell me?"

"You looked so happy," Marc said. "I didn't want to hurt you."

They looked at each other for a few seconds and then Lucy smiled.

"Promise me that next time you'll tell me," Lucy said. "No more secrets."

"I promise," Marc said.

"Good. So now you can tell me how you met Nathan and what his big secret is," Lucy laughed.

"That's not fair," Marc said.

But he told her the story. He told her that Nathan's dad was a famous rock star. A few years ago Nathan's dad received a phone call from a stranger. The stranger said he would kidnap[2] his son if he didn't pay a lot of money. His dad contacted[3] the police. Marc's mum was a police officer and Nathan came to stay at their home for a few weeks while they tried to catch the kidnappers[4]. Nathan went to school with Marc and they spent a lot of time together but Nathan couldn't say anything about his family or his past. They became great friends. It was a surprise when Marc discovered who Nathan's father was.

"That's a big secret," Lucy said. "I'd love to see Laura's face when she finds out!"

"Let's go to London now," Marc said. "We can still get to the theater in time for the afternoon rehearsals. And you can see Laura's face when Nathan tells her his secret.

It was the evening of the first performance and Dame Helen called everyone to the green room. Every theater

has a green room. It's the room where actors wait and relax[5] before or during a performance. No one knows why it's called the green room. Some people think it's because of the color of the walls but the walls of this green room were blue.

When Dame Helen and Bob entered[6] the room, all the actors and technicians[7] applauded. Dame Helen looked at everyone and smiled.

"This is an important night," she said. "You've all worked extremely hard and I know the show that you have created[8] will be a success. You're all very talented people and you should be proud of what you've achieved[9]. We have helped you as much as we can but now it's up to you[10]. Once the performance starts, our job is over."

---

1 apologetically [ə,pɑlə`dʒɛtɪkḷɪ] (adv.) 道歉地；認錯地
2 kidnap [`kɪdnæp] (v.) 綁架
3 contact [kən`tækt] (v.) 聯絡
4 kidnapper [`kɪdnæpɚ] (n.) 綁票者
5 relax [rɪ`læks] (v.) 放鬆
6 enter [`ɛntɚ] (v.) 進入
7 technician [tɛk`nɪʃən] (n.) 技術人員
8 create [krɪ`et] (v.) 創作
9 achieve [ə`tʃiv] (v.) 完成
10 It's up to you. 取決於你(們)。

Marc took out his notebook and started drawing the scene.

"Before you go on stage, I'd like to say one other thing," Dame Helen said. "I wanted to talk to you here in the green room because this is the place where actors are real people."

Dame Helen continued, "On stage you may be a duke, a shipwreck[1] survivor[2], a clown[3], or a sea captain[4]. But here in the green room, you're real people with real lives. Sometimes I think we expect[5] our lives to be as dramatic[6] and perfect as in a play. But our lives aren't written by William Shakespeare. And our stories don't always have happy endings[7]. I want you to remember—the person you are in the green room is much more important than the person you are on the stage. And the people you share your life with are more important than the characters you share the stage with. Now go out there and break a leg[8]!"

Laura, Nathan, Marc and Lucy walked down the stairs and along the corridor to the stage. They took it in turn[9] to look through the curtains at the audience. Marc's mum was there. Laura's mum and dad were sitting near the front. Nathan's dad was signing[10] autographs[11]. Even Lucy's mum and dad had agreed to stop arguing for one evening and come to the theater.

"This is your three-minute call[12]," the stage manager shouted. "Take your positions[13] for Act I Scene I."

"Let's meet in the green room in the interval[14]," Nathan said.

---

1 shipwreck [ˈʃɪpˌrɛk] (n.) 船隻遇難
2 survivor [səˈvaɪvɚ] (n.) 倖存者
3 clown [klaʊn] (n.) 小丑
4 sea captain 船長
5 expect [ɪkˈspɛkt] (v.) 期待
6 dramatic [drəˈmætɪk] (a.) 戲劇般的
7 happy ending 喜劇收場

8 break a leg〔劇場用語〕祝好運
9 in turn 輪流
10 sign [saɪn] (v.) 簽名
11 autograph [ˈɔtəˌgræf] (n.) 親筆簽名
12 three-minute call 最後倒數
13 take your position 就定位
14 interval [ˈɪntɚvl̩] (n.) 間隔

"Good idea," Laura said.

"Is anyone else nervous?" Lucy asked.

"I am," Marc said. "My hands are shaking and I'm not even acting!"

The four friends laughed. Marc took a last look at the scenery he had designed and painted. Nathan got in position for his entrance in the opening scene. And Laura and Lucy went to wait in the wings[1]. They heard the audience grow quiet as the lights dimmed[2]. Then there was a moment of total silence before the curtain rose[3]. Nathan walked onto the stage and spoke his first line.

"If music be the food of love, play on."

---

1 wing [wɪŋ] (n.) 側廳;廂房
2 dim [dɪm] (v.) 變暗
3 rise [raɪz] (v.) 上升 (動詞三態:rise; rose; risen)

AFTER READING

Ⓐ Personal Response

1 What did you think of the story? Write a paragraph describing your reaction to it.

2 Which of the four friends do you like most and why?

3 Did you think the characters were realistic?

4 Did you guess the end of the story before you finished reading?

5 Why do you think the story is called *The Green Room*?

6 Does the story remind you of any other books you have read or films or TV series you've watched? If so, which ones, and why?

7 Is there anything you would like to change in the story?

❸ Comprehension

1 Which of these adjectives describe Laura's feelings as she was waiting outside the theater for the auditions? Can you explain why?

- a nervous
- b funny
- c guilty
- d sad
- e stupid

2 For Nathan, what is "the most exciting place in the world"?

3 At the audition, why was everyone suddenly interested in Laura?

4 Who did Nathan do his audition scene with?

5 Why did Laura blush when Marc told Nathan that her mother was a famous film star?

6 Why did Laura change clothes on the train home?

7 Who phoned Marc in the middle of the night and why?

8 Where were Nathan, Laura and Marc when they received the good news from "The Green Room"?

9 Who was Lucy thinking about on the train to London on the first day of rehearsals?

10 Which picture did Marc draw in the auditorium before the rehearsals?

11 How did each day start during the rehearsals?

12 Why did some students find it difficult to read Shakespeare's words?

13 When was Lucy sure that Nathan was in love with her?

14 What did the students have to do when they met Bob on the stage for the first time?

15 Why did Marc and Nathan follow the girls on the train?

16 How did Lucy react when she discovered that Nathan didn't love her?

17 According to Nathan, why do the other kids at school want to be his friend?

18 What did Laura discover when she talked to her parents in Dame Helen's office?

19 How did Marc know how to find Lucy in the park when he went back to Hitchin?

20 With a partner write and act out the conversation between Marc and Lucy in the park.

ⓒ Characters

1 Choose the correct option.

    ⓐ Lucy went to the audition because she was jealous/proud of her friend.

    ⓑ Marc went to the audition because he wanted to/ Nathan told him to go.

    ⓒ Lucy thought that Laura's life was a thousand times better/worse than hers.

    ⓓ In Marc's dream, everything was made of paper/ plastic.

    ⓔ When Nathan's dad read the letter, he told his son it was good/bad news.

    ⓕ Marc wanted/didn't want to be an actor.

    ⓖ Nathan was/wasn't in love with Lucy.

2 What "secrets" do Laura and Nathan want to keep? Why?

3 In what ways are Lucy and Marc's lives similar?

4 Who says the following things? When do they say them and who do they say them to?

a "The person you are in the green room is much more important than the person you are on the stage. "

b " I don't understand why you don't tell your parents the truth. "

c " I think you're amazing, really, I do. But sometimes I feel as if I don't exist. "

d " I want you to close your eyes and run as fast as you can. "

e " You're my best friend. I know you better than you know yourself. "

f " I taught myself. "

g " You are normal, Nathan. Even I am normal, believe it or not. "

5 What can you remember about these characters? Write at least two things about each person.

a Jacquie ....

b Bob ....

c Marc's mum ....

d Laura's mum ....

❹ Plot and theme

1 Tick (✓) true (T) or false (F).

T **F** ⓐ Nathan is in love with Lucy.

T **F** ⓑ Laura lives in Pinewood.

T **F** ⓒ *Twelfth Night* and *What You Will* are both titles of the same play.

T **F** ⓓ Marc's parents are getting divorced.

T **F** ⓔ At first, Laura doesn't realize that Nathan is in love with her.

T **F** ⓕ Lucy told Dame Helen about Laura's lies.

T **F** ⓖ Dame Helen knew Laura's parents when they were younger.

2 In what way do Nathan and Laura change during the story?

3 Do you think the story has a message? If so, what is it?

4 Write the missing word in Bob's description of *Twelfth Night*.

It's about the mad things we think, see and do

when we are in ....

5 In what way is the plot of *Twelfth Night* similar to the main plot of the story?

6 Match this extract from the story with the Shakespeare quote that is closest in meaning.

> But sometimes people don't see what they should see. They only see what they want to see.

——— (a) "If music be the food of love, play on. Give me excess of it."

——— (b) "Shall I compare thee to a summer's day? Thou art more lovely and more temperate."

——— (c) "But love is blind and lovers cannot see the pretty follies that themselves commit."

7 What is method acting?

——— (a) A type of acting in which an actor becomes the character they are playing.

——— (b) A type of improvisation when an actor doesn't use a script.

——— (c) A type of acting exercise in which actors have to trust each other.

8 Who are your favorite female and male actors? Why do you like them?

9 What do you think are the advantages and disadvantages of having a famous parent?

10 Imagine you are the son or daughter of a famous person. Which famous person would you choose? How would your life be different?

E Language

1 Complete the sentences using the words below.

fan heart impression make-up
set soulmate tragedy

a When Marc talks to Nathan about Laura, he says, "You've found a ...."

b Jacquie is Nathan's dad's number one ....

c On the train, Laura put on some .... and then looked at herself in the mirror.

d Dame Helen said, "An audition is like meeting someone for the first time. You want to make a good ...."

e Nathan knew the whole speech by .... and everyone applauded when he reached the end.

f The opposite of a comedy is a ....

g Marc had the job of designing the ....

2 Nathan's dad doesn't know if you "go on the Net" or "go in the Net". Write the missing words in these sentences.

a Nathan searched for Laura .... the Internet.

b Laura picked .... the post as it fell through the letterbox.

c Dame Helen told them to never give .... hope.

d Marc took .... his notebook and started to draw a picture.

e Laura came back and sat .... opposite Lucy.

f They took it .... turns to stand in the spotlight and introduce their character.

3 Read and complete this extract from the story using either the noun of verb forms or "act" or "lie".

"I don't know how to (a)........................," Marc said.
"Of course you do,' Nathan laughed. 'Everyone (b)........................ all the time."
"I don't," Marc said.
"Don't you ever tell (c)........................ ?" Nathan asked.
"That's the same as (d)........................"
"No, I don't (e)........................," Marc said.
"I don't believe you. You're (f)........................!" Nathan laughed.

4 Write the verbs in brackets in the correct form.

(a) When Laura .... (leave) home in the morning, carrying her sports bag, she started walking towards Lucy's house.

(b) "Over the years," Dame Helen continued, "many of today's most successful theater, film and music stars .... (start) their careers here."

(c) At the end of the audition, Laura .... (send) a text message to her best friend, Lucy.

(d) In his dream, Marc .... (walk) down a street where everything was made of paper.

(e) The play is a comedy about mistaken identities and .... (start) with one of Shakespeare's most famous lines.

(f) Nathan and Marc often .... (see) people following other people in spy films and TV series but it was more difficult in real life.

(g) Laura suddenly .... (feel) embarrassed and angry. She turned and walked out of the rehearsal room.

(h) "It .... (not be) easy being the son of one of the most famous rock musicians in the world," he thought.

TEST

⭐ **1** Look at the text in each question.
Then choose the correct answer.

a What does it say?

1. You may not queue before the theater opens.
2. Please queue inside the theater.
3. You may queue outside the theater until it opens.

STUDENTS MUST QUEUE HERE. THEATER OPENS AT 11.

b What should Lucy do?

1. Buy Laura's ticket and wait on the platform.
2. Meet Laura on the train with her ticket.
3. Not buy Laura's ticket but wait on the platform.

See you at the train station. I will be late so please buy my train ticket and I'll meet you on the platform. Laura

c What does Bob say?

1. The students are happy working in the normal place.
2. The students would like to try working in a smaller room.
3. The students would like to have more space.

Can we use the stage for rehearsals today? The students want to practice with more space.
Bob

d When is a good time to buy tickets?

1. On Monday morning.
2. At lunch time.
3. On Saturday afternoon.

Tickets to "The Green Room" summer school's production can be bought from the ticket office, open Monday to Friday from 9 am to 6 pm.
Closed for lunch from 1 pm to 2p m.

P 2 Read the extract from the story and choose the correct word for each space. Write 1, 3, 3 or 4 in the space.

Marc (a) .... Lucy that Nathan's dad was a famous rock star. A few years ago Nathan's dad (b) .... a phone call from a stranger. The stranger said he would (c) .... his son if he didn't pay (d) .... money. His dad contacted the police. Marc's mum was a police officer and Nathan came to stay at their home (e) .... a few weeks while they tried to catch the kidnappers. Nathan went to school with Marc and they spent a lot of time together but Nathan (f) .... say anything about his family or his past. They became (g) .... friends. It was a surprise when Marc discovered (h) .... Nathan's father was.

_____	a	1 says	2 said	3 tell	4 told
_____	b	1 made	2 received	3 was	4 get
_____	c	1 kidnap	2 kidnapping	3 to kidnap	4 kidnapped
_____	d	1 a lot of	2 very	3 many	4 a lot
_____	e	1 with	2 since	3 from	4 for
_____	f	1 could	2 not	3 couldn't	4 never
_____	g	1 very	2 so	3 great	4 with
_____	h	1 why	2 who	3 where	4 which

3 In pairs choose two different pictures in the book. Take turns telling each other what you can see in your picture.

I can see...

Is there...?

01 Improvise

In groups of three, prepare an audition scene in which two of you are parents and one of you is their teenage son or daughter. It is twelve o'clock at night and the son or daughter has just arrived home. The parents don't know where their son or daughter has been and they have been worried.

02 Read

Download Act V Scene I from *Twelfth Night* from our website. In groups of three, choose one of the parts and read from the script. Perform the scene in class.

Web

03 Write

What happens to the characters in *The Green Room*?
Imagine it is five years later and Laura, Nathan, Lucy
and Marc meet again. Where do they meet? What do
they say to each other? What has happened to them?
Write a short scene, then rehearse and perform it in
front of the other students in the class.

作者簡介

羅伯，你好，可以跟我們介紹一下你自己嗎？

我在威爾斯出生，在蘇格蘭長大，目前旅居西班牙，致力於寫作。這是我為 Helbling Languages 公司所寫的第三本讀本。

這篇故事的靈感是怎麼來的？

《男孩女孩的夏日劇場學園》講的是幾個少年男女在劇場暑期營的故事。我在少年時代，夢想著能夠當一名演員，曾經加入了「國家年輕人劇場」（National Youth Theater）。這個組織鼓勵 14 到 21 歲的青少年們學習戲劇，有很多演員都是從這裡出來的，像是奧蘭多·布魯、丹尼爾·克雷格、丹尼爾·戴-路易斯、海倫·米蘭、馬特·史密斯。

我的處女作是《Zigger Zagger》，內容講述足球迷的故事。那是一次神奇的經驗，於是我決定要寫一篇時下青少年們的普遍經驗。

你曾經當過職業演員嗎？

不曾，我沒那麼厲害！不過之後的幾年，我為國家年輕人劇場的戲做了一些音樂，並擔任過音樂指導。在我開始寫小說之前，我為很多戲劇編寫過音樂和歌曲，其中有一齣戲還是講述本書中會提到的演員詹姆士·狄恩的故事。

這篇故事有想要傳達什麼嗎？

當然有囉，不過，這得靠你自己來閱讀尋找了。

Part 1 試鏡

1. 蘿拉

P.13

「我幹嘛來這裡啊？」蘿拉一邊自問，眼神一邊越過前面一位男孩的肩膀延頸觀望。

劇場外面的青少年大排長龍，蘿拉排在最後一個。

「這裡最少有八十個人。」她想。

這天是星期六上午，蘿拉緊張不已地排隊等著進劇場。她心裡還有一些些罪惡感，因為她在吃早餐時跟爸媽撒了謊。

「你要去哪？」爸爸問。

「去露西家。我們有一個考試要準備，然後去練游泳。」蘿拉說。

「你會比較晚回來嗎？」媽媽問。

「不一定。我會再打電話回來，好嗎？」

這件事露西是知道的，以免蘿拉的爸媽打電話找露西。露西是蘿拉最要好的朋友，都會幫忙罩她。

蘿拉早上背上運動包包出門後，便往露西家的方向走去，等她來到了大馬路，才反方向地向左轉，然後快步走向火車站。十點零三分有一班火車，到倫敦的車程只要半個鐘頭，所以有寬裕的時間可以在十一點以前趕到劇場。

P.14

上了火車之後，她帶著包包去洗手間換上另外一套衣服——紅色的上衣可以讓她顯眼一些，這件牛仔褲是她最好的牛仔褲，而這雙新鞋子是她上個週末才和露西一起去買的。她還上了點妝。她看著鏡子裡的自己，這樣跟自己打氣說，「你一定可以做得到的！」

蘿拉在火車上時還自信滿滿，可是現在來到劇場門外卻退縮了起來，而且感到罪惡感。

「我幹嘛來這裡啊？」蘿拉又自問了一遍。這一次她才意識到自己的聲音有點大聲，因為前面的男孩這時轉過身來盯著她看。

「你是在跟我講話嗎？」戴眼鏡的男孩問。

這下子，蘿拉不只覺得緊張、有罪惡感，而且還覺得自己很蠢。她想衝回國王十字火車站，搭上最近的一班火車回家。不過這時她看到了男孩手裡拿著的筆記本，他正在畫青少年們在劇場外面大排長龍的畫面。

蘿拉不禁笑了笑。

「你畫得不賴嘛。」她說。

「謝啦。」她說。

「我叫蘿拉。」她說。

「我叫馬可，字母是 C 的『可』，和馬可·夏卡爾的一樣。」

蘿拉聽了沒有多加回應，馬可於是又說道：「是那個畫家？」

「我知道馬可·夏卡爾是誰。」蘿拉唬弄道。

馬可笑了笑，蘿拉這時才又感到自信。

「他竟然相信了，可見我的演技真的很好吧。」她想。

2. 納森

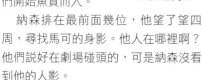

P.16

十一點零五分，門終於打開了，青少年們開始魚貫而入。

納森排在最前面幾位，他望了望四周，尋找馬可的身影。他人在哪裡啊？他們說好在劇場碰頭的，可是納森沒看到他的人影。

納森坐在劇場觀眾席上的第一排，深深地呼吸著。他很喜歡劇場的味道，每次只要去劇場，他就會有這樣的感覺。這種感覺難以形容，有點像是離家多年之後再度返家的感覺。對納森來說，劇場是世界上最令他興奮的地方。在這裡，什麼事情都可能上演。

幾分鐘後，一位女士走上舞台，大家於是開始鼓掌。那是海倫夫人，她是「綠房」的導演，也是國內知名的演員。她舉起手，現場頓時安靜下來。

「感謝各位來參加綠房夏日劇場學園的試鏡。我想各位都知道，我們每年都會有幾百位來自全國各地的青少年來試鏡，大家的年齡都在十五歲和十七歲之間。通過今天的試鏡的人，暑假將會留在倫敦這裡，和職業級的導演、演員、音樂家一起共事。你們將會學習演戲、舞蹈和歌唱，並且參與本劇場今年度的演出，地點就在這個舞台上，面對著真正的觀眾。」

試鏡

- 這些青少年們是要參加什麼樣的試鏡？
- 你曾經參加過試鏡嗎？試鏡會讓你很緊張嗎？

P.17

納森剎那間覺得自己就正站在台上，站在海倫夫人的旁邊，對著數百名的觀眾做表演。

「這麼多年來，有許多時下最成功的劇場明星、電影明星或是歌星，就是從這個舞台上開始發跡的。他們也曾坐在各位現在所坐的位置上，緊張地等候他們第一次的試鏡。」

海倫夫人停了一會兒，納森覺得她對他笑了一下。

「試鏡，就好像要和某人初次見面一樣，你一心想留下好印象，卻往往事與願違。我們每個人都不一樣，如果你這一次沒有幸運地通過，也不要因此放棄希望。從這次的經驗中學習，對自己要有信心。祝各位好運了。」

海倫夫人笑了笑，走下舞台，現場一片掌聲和歡呼。

接下來，出現了四位助理。他們把所有的人分成四組，然後分別帶到劇場的不同角落裡。

納森跟著小組離開觀眾席，沿著走廊走下去，然後走上一個迴旋梯，蜿蜒來到劇場的頂樓，那裡有一個金屬製的大門，上面掛著「禁止進入」的招牌。

「就是這裡了。」他一邊走進大門，一邊想道。

3. 馬可

P.18

在劇場的另一個角落，馬可站在一間擠滿人的大房間裡。一個留著紅髮、蓄著紅鬍子的年輕男人，正坐在一張椅子上。

「請大家注意，請在地板上找個位置坐下來。」年輕人說。

馬可在房間的後方找了一個位置坐下，將背靠在牆面上。房間裡沒有任何擺設，除了一面牆上裝設了幾面長鏡子之外。馬可戴上眼鏡想尋找納森，但沒找著。他大概在別的小組裡，現在在劇場的另一個角落吧。接著，他看到蘿拉就坐在房間的中間地方，他向她招手，但她沒有看到他。

紅髮男子這時拍手要大家注意。

「各位，聽好了，我叫鮑伯。」他停了一下，讓現場安靜下來之後，繼續說道：「我想先請每一個人起立發言，跟我們大家介紹一下你自己，並且講一下你為什麼會來這裡的原因。」

馬可想隱身起來。他不喜歡講自己的事。他拿出筆記本，開始畫最先起立發言的人。那是一個十五歲的女孩，名字叫珍。她之所以會來這裡，是因為她一心想成為一名舞者。馬可看得出來她非常緊張，因為她兩手緊握地站著，眼睛只敢看地板。

P.20

接下來，起立的是蘿拉。她比珍來得有自信，她先是直視鮑伯的眼睛，然後再看看周圍的人，幾秒鐘之後才開始發言。

「我叫蘿拉，我跟媽媽住在松塢，我的父親已經過世。我們家離電影製片廠很近，我之所以來這裡，是因為我想像我媽那樣，成為一位知名的演員。」

大家聽了耳朵都豎了起來。

「你媽媽是……？」鮑伯問蘿拉。

「我想，這還是不要說的比較好。」蘿拉說。

自信

- 蘿拉是如何表現得比珍更有自信的？
- 你有自信嗎？
- 你覺得自信心很重要嗎？

鮑伯點頭笑了笑。接著換一個男孩站起來自我介紹。很快地，房間裡其他的所有人都輪流起立發言，最後只剩下一個人。

「你是哪一位呢？」鮑伯問。

馬可緊張地站起身來。

「我叫馬可。」他溫溫地回答。

「那麼，馬可，你為什麼會來這裡呢？」鮑伯問。

「是納森叫我來的。」馬可說。

房間裡所有的人都笑了出來。馬可的臉一陣發燙。他看了一下蘿拉，蘿拉也在笑。

「只要納森叫你做什麼，你就會去做嗎？」鮑伯問。

P.21

鮑伯走到馬可站的地方，把他的筆記本拿了起來，開始翻閱他的繪畫。

「畫得很好啊。你是在哪裡學畫畫的？」鮑伯問。

「我是自己學的。」馬可回答。

鮑伯點了點頭，然後拍手大聲說道：「好了，各位，請大家分成三個小組，我會給你們一個情境，然後請大家設計場景，然後在海倫夫人的面前表演。可以嗎？」

4. 納森

P.22

在劇場的頂樓房間，納森和他的小組正在海倫夫人的面前做試鏡。他在試鏡的場景中和一個女孩演對手戲。他們在場景中飾演一對父母，他們要即興演出一段為未成年女兒在起爭執的戲碼。時間是設定在晚上十一點，這對父母還在等女兒回家。

納森不知道要怎麼起頭，但那個女孩很清楚如何開頭。

「每次都是我在收拾殘局！」她很生氣地對納森說。

「你這話什麼意思？」納森問。他很驚訝，那個女孩的言語和動作真的很像做媽媽的。女孩繼續說道：「你整天都在外面工作，回家後就只會坐在電視機面前，看電視看到睡著。你不和我說話，也不和女兒說話！」

「你亂講。」納森說。

「她在學校曠課，你有找她談嗎？她被警察帶回來，你有找她談嗎？你上一次找她講話是什麼時候的事了？」女孩說。

納森不知道要如何接，他張開嘴巴，吐不出話來。還好，大家以為這是表演的一部分。這時他靈機一動。

「還不就是你太愛嘮叨了，不知道閉嘴！你老愛嫌她，這個不能做，那裡不能去，這個不能穿，那種人不要跟他見面。你應該要給她一些喘息的空間，讓我們父女的耳根清靜一下！」

5. 蘿拉

P.23

停頓了片刻之後，換女孩說。

女孩接著說：「等她回來，我就找她談。」

「別再談了！」納森大聲喊道。

這一場戲結束之後，房間裡響起一片熱烈的掌聲。海倫笑了笑，說：「很好！」

納森和女孩坐了下來，他的身體還餘顫未了。

「你好厲害啊，表演得好真實。」他對女孩說。

「謝啦，你也不賴啊。」女孩說。這時她的包包裡傳出嗡嗡的聲音。她拿出手機，讀了一則簡訊後，露出了愁容。

「沒事吧？」納森問。

「沒事，是我死黨傳的簡訊。她不知道我來這裡，她要是知道了，一定會不高興的。」

P.24

試鏡結束後，蘿拉傳了一則簡訊給好友露西，她寫道：「一切都很酷，待會見。」試鏡很順利。蘿拉提到媽媽是知名演員，讓大家留下了印象，而且鮑伯和海倫夫人也都很喜歡她的試鏡表演。當她尾隨馬可進入走廊上時，她可以感覺人們在盯著她看，她還聽到有人說：「你猜她媽媽是誰？」

在劇場大廳裡，所有的青少年們都在談試鏡的事，個個有說有笑的。蘿拉掏出手機，查看露西回覆的簡訊。「待會兒，比你想得更快！」

蘿拉一開始意會不過來，接著她才開始在大廳裡尋找熟悉的面孔。她快步穿過人群，來到納森和演對手戲女孩所站立的地方。

「露西！你怎麼會在這裡？」蘿拉問女孩。

露西一時不知如何回答，緊張地笑了笑。

「嗨，蘿拉。」她說。

「露西？你怎麼會在這裡？」蘿拉又問了一次。

「我就很羨慕你啊！」露西說：「你一直在說試鏡的事，所以我自己也想來試試。」她轉頭向納森說：「看吧，她沒有很高興，是吧？」

馬可這時朝著他們群聚的地方走過來。

「嗨，納森。」馬可說。

「馬可，你去哪裡了呀？我一直在找你。」納森問道。

馬可轉向蘿拉說道：「嗨，蘿拉，這是我朋友，納森。」

P.26

「就是那位有名的納森啊。」蘿拉笑了笑，一時忘記了露西的事，「是你叫馬可一定要來試鏡的。」

「你才有名了呢。」馬可跟蘿拉說。

「有名？」納森突然對蘿拉產生興趣地問道。

「她媽媽是一位知名的電影明星。」馬可回答。

蘿拉的臉一陣羞紅地看著露西。

「我在試鏡上跟他們說我媽媽的事。」蘿拉說。

露西緩緩地點了點頭說：「我知道了。」

蘿拉想轉移話題，於是跟馬可介紹露西。

「馬可，這是露西，我最要好的朋友。我不知道她也來試鏡了。」蘿拉說。

「很意——外吧！」露西刻意想要寶一下。

「露西很會演耶。」納森說。

「你也住在松塢嗎？」馬可問露西。

在露西還來不及回答之前，蘿拉連忙說他們得走了。

「我們要是再不走，就會趕不上火車啦。」她緊張地說。

她抓著露西的手，跟大家說再見。兩個女孩之後走出劇場。

「我有說錯話嗎？」馬可問。

納森聳聳肩說：「不知。」

認識新朋友

- 露西、蘿拉、馬可、納森初次見面，是誰引介誰？他們各自說了什麼話？
- 和夥伴們分成四人一組，來練習互相介紹朋友。

6. 露西

P.27

露西坐在火車上，注視著窗外。蘿拉在洗手間換回平時週末會穿的衣服，並且卸妝。露西的腦子裡都是納森，他真的說她很會演戲嗎？她覺得他也很會演啊。她回想納森跟大家自我介紹的樣子時，笑了出來。「嗨，我叫納森，凡夫一枚。我和我爸住在倫敦，過著平凡的生活。我之所以會來這裡，是因為我熱愛戲劇，想成為一位演員。」

蘿拉這時走回來坐在露西的對面。這兩個好朋友互相注視了一會兒，彼此默

不作聲。後來蘿拉開口道：「露西，我還是很難相信。你怎麼也跑去試鏡了？我跟我爸媽說我是跟你在一起的。」

「我也有我自己的夢想。」露西回答。

「沒有，你沒有。」蘿拉說。

「你怎麼就知道？」露西問。

「因為我很了解你。你是我最好的朋友，我比你還了解你自己。」蘿拉說。

「你才不了解我呢！你一點都不了解我，你只知道你自己，你永遠只會聊自己的事。你只聊你自己，都是你、你、你。」露西生氣地說。

露西再度面向窗外，她覺得窗戶的玻璃上閃現了一下納森的臉，然後消失不見。露西回過頭來看著蘿拉。

P.29

「你到底是怎麼跟他們說你媽媽的？」露西問。

「也沒什麼，我只是跟他們說我媽是一位知名的演員。」

「你還跟他們說了什麼？」露西問。

「我說我們住在松塢。」蘿拉說。

「松塢在哪裡？」露西問。

「我也不知道，那裡有製片廠，詹姆士‧龐德的電影都是在那邊拍攝的。」她停了一下，「還有，我想我說了我爸已經過世的話。」

「哦，蘿拉！」露西說。她的口氣聽起來彷彿對朋友很失望似的。

幾分鐘後，火車進入了希金站。兩個女孩下了車。他們一起在大馬路上走著，最後蘿拉向右拐彎走回家。

「再見。」蘿拉說。

「再見。」露西說。

露西看著她的朋友沿著街道走下去。蘿拉為什麼要騙說她媽媽的事？為什麼要說她爸爸已經過世？為什麼她騙別人說她住在哪裡？難道蘿拉在現實生活中真的過得很不快樂？露西覺得蘿拉身在福中不知福，她的生活比她好上一千倍。她舉步走回家，希望回去不會又聽到父母在吵架。

7. 馬可

P.30

現在是凌晨兩點，手機響的時候，馬可已經睡著了。他那時正在做一個夢，夢到自己在街上走著，所有的東西都是紙做的，房子是紙做的，車子是紙做的，連人也是紙做的。馬可這時看了一下自己的雙手，他的手也是紙做的。就在這時，紙做的手機響起，吵醒了馬可。他伸手拿起手機。

「喂？」馬可看了一下是誰打來的電話，但他沒有戴眼鏡，看不清楚字幕。「誰啊？」

「我睡不著。」納森在電話那頭說道。

「那你為什麼要把我吵起來，跟我說

你睡不著？」馬可說。

「不是啦，我想請你跟我說說蘿拉的事。」納森說。

「她的什麼事？」

「我也不知道。她是什麼樣的人？」

「蘿拉？」馬可一邊說，一邊回想女孩在劇場外面排隊的時候，回想她說她媽媽是知名演員，還有她拉著露西跑出劇場的樣子。「我也不知道，我覺得她有一點……怪怪的。」

「怪怪的？」納森說：「我喜歡她耶，我沒辦法不想她。」

馬可笑了出來。

「那是因為她媽媽很有名，對吧？」馬可說。

「才不是呢，不是這樣的，」納森撒謊說，「好吧，大概有一點點啦。」

「你找到自己的靈魂伴侶啦。」馬可說。

「什麼意思？」納森問。

「同是天涯淪落人啊。」

「你不會跟他們說吧？馬可？你在嗎？這是祕密，對吧？你答應我？」納森說。

「我答應你。快睡吧，納森。」馬可說。

8. 納森，蘿拉，露西，馬可

三個星期之後。納森這時在倫敦家中的廚房裡作早餐。

「爸！早餐好囉！」他大聲喊道。

納森的爸爸不會弄吃的。他只會吃，不會做飯。午餐和晚餐通常是賈桂煮的，早餐則一直都是由納森負責。賈桂是爸的頭號粉絲，她總是說：「我是你的頭號粉絲。」

「早啊，納森。」爸爸一邊走進廚房，一邊說道：「聞起來好香啊。」

「嗨，爸，是你最喜歡的吐司夾蛋。」納森說。

「你怎麼沒去學校？」爸爸問。

「爸，今天星期六。」

「星期六？對喔！」納森的爸爸在餐桌旁邊坐下來之後，開始拆一小疊信件。「你有『去』網了嗎？」他問。

「是『上』網，爸，是『上網』。」

「所以才說『網路』，而不是『網線』？」

「很好笑，爸。」納森說：「我把你的電子郵件印出來了，放在你的書桌上。」

「人們怎就不放過我？」納森的爸爸一邊問，一邊打開了一封信。

「因為他們都愛你啊，爸。」納森坐在餐桌上，一邊吃著早餐，一邊說道。

「這封信是你的，是綠房寄來的。」爸爸看了一下拿起來的第二封信，說道。

納森的爸爸把信抽出來拿給他，但納森沒有接過信。

「爸，你幫我拆信，我太緊張了。」納森説。

納森的爸爸於是拆開信封，取出信紙。他開始看信，表情一路跟著改變，神情很嚴肅。

「怎樣？信裡頭寫什麼？」納森問。

P.34

「恐怕不是個好消息。」爸爸説。

「喔。」納森失望地説。

「抱歉啦，納森，你暑假只能留在倫敦，因為你要去上戲劇課啦！你被錄取啦，納森！」

「爸！」納森叫道，他到底要相信哪一個啊。

納森接過信，開始讀信。爸爸説的沒錯，納森的試鏡通過了，綠房的夏日劇場學園已經給他安插了位置。

在五十五哩外的希金，蘿拉跑去前門拿從信箱掉進來的信件。她在等綠房寄來的通知，所以這是她每天早上必做的事情。她可不想讓爸媽看到通知。他們不知道她去倫敦的事情，她知道他們一定不想讓她去參加夏日劇場學園。

今天，通知終於寄來了。她從地板上拾起通知，放進口袋裡，然後直衝到樓上的房間。就在她把信封拆開之際，她的手機響了起來。是露西打來的。

「嗨，蘿拉，你收到通知了嗎？」露西問。

「我才正準備打開信，你呢？」

「我也是。」露西説。

蘿拉從信封內抽出信紙，很快地讀了起來。

P.35

> 　　　　　　　　　綠房
> 　　　　　　　貝福廣場
> 　　　　　　　　　倫敦
>
> 五月二日星期三
>
> 親愛的蘿拉您好：
>
> 　　很感謝您來倫敦參加綠房夏日劇場學園的試鏡。很高興通知您，您的申請加入已經核准，恭喜您！
>
> 　　您可以在我們的網站上找到更多暑期課程的資料，包括在倫敦住宿的資訊，如果您有需要的話。
>
> 　　參加綠房，需要您父母的同意書，在排演的第一天，請帶上您父母的同意書前來。
>
> 　　期待暑假與您在倫敦相見！
>
> 誠摯的祝福
>
> 鮑伯·哈林頓
> 副導

「上面寫什麼？」露西問。

「我通過了！我要去倫敦了！」蘿拉盡量小聲地説道，以免被爸媽聽到。

「我也是耶！」露西在電話上叫喊道。

「我上班快遲到了！」馬可的媽媽一邊看著廚房桌子上的信件，一邊説道：「你不把信開來看嗎？」

「何必呢？裡頭一定是寫説我不適合演戲。」馬可説。

這講得沒錯，馬可不適合演戲，而他也不想當什麼演員的。有演員夢的是納森，馬可去參加試鏡，純粹是納森拉他一起去的。他記得他當時和納森的對話。

「我又不會演戲。」馬可説。

「你當然會啊，人都嘛在演戲。」納森笑道。

「我沒有。」馬可説。

「你沒有説過謊話嗎？」納森問，「演戲就是這麼一回事。」

「我沒説過謊。」馬可説。

「我才不信，你騙人！」納森笑了起來。

「你不會演戲無所謂啊，你是個藝術家，一個很有天分的藝術家。」媽媽説。

「謝啦，媽。」

馬可的媽媽在鏡子裡照了照。

「要不要我幫你看信？」她問。

馬可看了一下穿著帥氣黑白警察制服的媽媽。

「這是危險任務。」馬可裂開嘴笑著。

媽媽在他的臉頰上親吻了一下，然後出門上班。聽到前門被關上的聲音後，馬可這才細心地拆起信。

　　親愛的馬可：

　　很感謝您來倫敦參加綠房夏日劇場學園的試鏡。很抱歉通知您，您的申請加入未通過核准，希望您不會太失望！然而，我們認為您的繪畫很出色，所以想在我們的技術團隊中幫您安插一個職務，幫忙這次的暑假檔設計場景和戲服。希望您能接受這項安排。

馬可不敢相信自己的眼睛，於是又把信讀了一遍。他們請他去倫敦耶。

「太好啦！」他喊道。

信件

• 這四位朋友收到什麼樣的信件？
• 信件的內容對他們來說意謂著什麼？
• 他們四個人這個暑假會做什麼？
• 你收過什麼很重要的信件嗎？

Part 2 排演

9. 蘿拉，露西

P.39

今天是排演的第一天，蘿拉和露西正坐在前往倫敦的火車上。

「你怎麼跟你爸媽說的？」露西問。

「我跟他們說學校有一個全國巡迴的校際游泳比賽，我說我每天都要練習，而且會巡迴各地。」蘿拉說。

「他們相信？」露西說。

「當然了，」蘿拉說：「我是個演員。」

「那同意書呢？要帶上的父母同意書呢？」露西問。

蘿拉笑了笑，從運動包包掏出一個信封。

「媽媽寫了參加游泳比賽的同意書，我昨天晚上另外描了一份，然後把游泳比賽改成劇場學校。一份完美的偽造文書。」

「真不懂你為什麼不跟你爸媽直說。」露西說。

P.40

「因為他們不會懂的，他們只懂他們那種無聊的生活，要我也跟他們過一樣無聊的生活。我才不想跟他們一樣，我想要特別一點的生活。你有跟你爸媽講嗎？」

露西望著窗外。「有啊，不過他們不會管我在做什麼。我整個暑假都不會待在家裡，他們很高興就是了。這樣他們就有更多的時間吵架啦。」

「有時候，我倒希望我爸媽多吵一點架。」蘿拉說。

「別這麼說，千萬別這麼說。我喜歡你爸媽，他們在一起的樣子好幸福。你應該跟他們說實話的。夜路走多了會遇到鬼。」

謊言

- 列出蘿拉所說過的謊言。你覺得她為什麼要說謊？
- 你是否有時候也會撒這種謊？為什麼？

蘿拉用嚴肅的表情看著好友。

「你什麼都不會說的，對吧？如果有人問起，就說我和知名的演員媽媽住在松塢，爸爸已經過世。」她說。

「幻想自己有一個出名的媽媽，你想這樣大家就真的會認為你與眾不同嗎？你媽要姓什麼？瓊斯，跟你一樣？」露西說。

「她成名之後就換了姓，還有，不要忘了你也住在松塢。」蘿拉說。

P.41

「不要，我才不要瞎掰自己的事。你想的話你可以住在松塢，但我住在希金。」露西說。

「可是你是我最好的朋友，如果我們住在不同的地方，別人會覺得很奇怪。」

「不要，我不要。」露西說。

他們快抵達倫敦了。露西望著窗外，看著沿途的房子。

「不知道納森住在哪裡。」她暗忖道。

10. 納森，馬可

P.43

納森和馬可來到劇場後，他們穿過觀眾席。現場大約有三十名青少年，納森和馬可認出試鏡上見過的一些人，不過也有些是陌生的面孔。

「她在哪裡啊？」納森一邊張望，一邊問道，「蘿拉在哪裡啊？」

「可能試鏡沒有通過吧。」馬可說。他拿出筆記本，開始畫納森站在舞台上，手裡捧著一顆破碎的心。然後又畫一顆大大的破碎的心，在旁邊寫上：「N 愛 L」。

「我又不愛她。」納森看著繪畫，一邊說道。

「不愛？你從那天試鏡之後，滿口講的都是她。」馬可說。

「她有一點不一樣嘛，她就……那樣不一樣嘛。」納森說。

「你也不一樣嘛，對吧？你終有一天要跟她坦白的。」馬可說。

「坦白什麼？」納森問。

「你爸的事啊。」馬可說。

「這是祕密，不可以跟任何人說，你答應過的。」納森生氣地說。

蘿拉和露西這時走進了觀眾席，納森瞬間容光煥發。他向她們招手，兩個女孩於是向他們走過來，在男孩們的旁邊坐了下來。他們聊著通知書的事，有說有笑的。這時，露西看到了馬可筆記本上畫的納森。

P.44

「你在畫什麼？」露西問馬可。

「沒什麼。」馬可一邊回答，一邊很快把筆記本闔起來。

不過為時已晚，露西看到了納森破碎的心旁邊寫著「N 愛 L」。「納森愛露西。」她想。

之後，試鏡上那位紅髮的年輕人鮑伯現身在舞台上，歡迎同學們來到綠房。

「今天，你們大家就要展開這一次的旅程了。這不是一次輕鬆的旅程，過程中有些人可能會離開。不過只要你們做好準備，認真努力，大家一起打拚，那麼這一次的旅程將讓各位畢生難忘。大家準備好要開始了嗎？」他說。

觀眾席上的每一個人都大聲回應道：「準備好了！」

「我聽不到！」鮑伯喊道。

「準備好了！」大家又大聲喊了一遍。

旅程

• 鮑伯講的「旅程」是指什麼？

• 你有參加過類似的旅程嗎？

• 想一想，有什麼字可以用來形容這趟旅程？

11. 鮑伯

P.46

　　鮑伯很樂在喊喊叫叫之中。在前幾天，綠房夏日劇場學園很像軍事學校，每天早上九點鐘，便會以熱身操揭開一天的序幕。首先，每個人先站立好，然後搖身體，把自己搖醒。接著，鮑伯會大聲下指令，要大家做伏地挺身和仰臥起坐，再接下來是呼吸和發音練習。鮑伯很樂在其中，因為他可以在發號施令的同時發出一些怪聲怪調的聲音。大家都要張嘴做出各種奇奇怪怪的嘴形，然後模仿鮑伯所發出的聲音。再來大家就要又喊又唱，做出更多奇怪的聲音，直到鮑伯喊「停」。

　　在做完熱身操之後，接下來是戲劇課。上戲劇課時，學生會被分成三個小組。鮑伯會負責其中一個小組，另外兩個小組由另外兩位老師帶。在第一週，他們做了很多「信任感的練習」。鮑伯說，演員彼此之間的相互信任是非常重要的。鮑伯最喜歡的信任感練習叫做「小雞快跑」。

　　「現在，各位，我們需要大空間來練習。」鮑伯說。

　　大家於是把椅子搬到房間的一邊，這是一個長形的房間，兩邊有鏡子，鏡子可以讓房間看起來大一些。鮑伯首先要大家先靠牆邊站，然後請一個人自告奮勇。納森於是站了出來。

P.47

　　「很好，納森，請你走到房間的另外一頭。」鮑伯說。

　　納森於是走到長形房間的另外一頭，面向站在對面牆前的大家。

P.48

　　「現在，納森，請聽仔細了，我要你閉上眼睛，然後用你最快的速度，對著房間另一邊的牆跑過去。你不會有事的，在你撞到牆之前，我們會攔住你。」他看著另一邊的人，「沒錯吧？我們會攔住納森。」然後又轉過頭來看納森，「你要做的事，就是閉上眼睛，用你最快的速度奔跑，信任我們每一個人。這你能做得到嗎？」

　　納森不確定自己能否信任每一個人，但他知道他非照做不可。於是他抽一口氣，閉上眼睛，開始快跑。閉上眼睛快跑的感覺很奇怪，他一開始覺得自己會撞到東西或是撞到人。不過在別人還沒開始攔住之前，他很快就放開來了。

　　鮑伯跟大家說，他稱這種練習叫做「小雞快跑」，這個名字來自《養子不教

誰之過》這部老片的一場戲。

在電影中，有兩個青少年開車衝向懸崖，然後在車子衝下懸崖之前，跳出車子。其中一個人跳出了車子，但另外一個人並沒有成功。

「這部電影由詹姆斯·狄恩主演，他的演戲方式是『融入法』，有人知道什麼是融入法嗎？」鮑伯說。

P.49

納森舉起手。

「那是一種演戲的方法，演員要投入變成劇中的角色。」納森說。

「沒錯。你不可以只是把劇本的台詞唸出來而已，而是要融入角色裡，把那些話講出來。你的思想、你的舉止，都會變成那個角色。」

房間後方這時傳出了一個女孩的笑聲。

「如果你的角色是一位殺手，那怎麼辦？難道要去殺人嗎？」她問。

「當然不是了，不過你得進入殺手的內心世界，去找出來那位殺手為什麼會變成殺手的原因，他的人生有過什麼經歷，有時候可能是很駭人的經驗。這也是你們必須信任彼此的原因。」鮑伯說。

演戲
•演員在演戲時應該如何演出？
•他們必須信任誰？
•你參與過任何演出嗎？

12. 納森

P.50

到了下午，所有的學生都要練習日後要上演的戲碼。馬可和技術組在一起，當其他人在做排演時，他們在設計場景和戲服。今年度綠房要上演的戲碼叫做《隨心所欲》。在第一個下午，海倫夫人跟大家介紹了這齣戲。

「《隨心所欲》是威廉·莎士比亞劇本《第十二夜》的另一個劇名，我們打算將這個劇本做一個另類的演出。我們會以莎士比亞的故事和角色開啟序幕，之後再加上我們自己的台詞、音樂和舞蹈。」她說。

海倫夫人還說，明天會是角色分配的日子，她說選角是當演員的另一個重要關鍵。當導演在為劇本或是電影選角時，他們會為各個角色或人物找出合適的演員人選。

納森知道，如果他想要得到一個好的劇中角色，就必須先做一些功課。他當天晚上回到家後，便進了自己的房間下載了莎士比亞的原劇劇本《第十二

夜》，並且搜尋了一些資料。他發現莎士比亞的這個劇本約寫於 1601 年。

P.51

這是一齣身分錯亂的喜劇，以莎士比亞的名句開啟序幕——「如果音樂是愛情的糧食，那麼就演奏下去吧。」這第一句對白是由劇中人物歐西諾所說。納森一開始讀劇本，就立刻知道自己很想飾演歐西諾這個角色。

隔天下午，海倫夫人和鮑伯要學生先讀莎士比亞劇本的綱要。

有些人覺得莎士比亞的英文不是很好懂，十七世紀人們所講的英語很不一樣，有很多字現在都變成古字了，而且莎士比亞還是用韻文寫成的。

P.52

露西是不錯，納森心想，但蘿拉更好。接下來，輪到納森來試這句話。

「如果音樂是愛情的糧食，那麼就演奏下去吧。」他說，「就給我過量的，好讓愛情因為過飽噎塞而死吧。」納森整段對白都背了下來，當他結束時，每一個人都給他掌聲。

「我想我們已經找到歐西諾了。」海倫夫人說。

隔天早上，卡司表已經釘在布告欄上了。納森獲得了歐西諾的角色，蘿拉獲得了菲兒拉的角色，露西獲得了奧莉薇的角色。這三個朋友分別拿到了劇本中最主要的三個角色。

13. 露西，馬可

P.53

第四天，露西在前往排演的途中，看到了馬可坐在劇場旁邊的咖啡廳裡。她走進咖啡廳，在他面前坐了下來。馬可這時埋首在筆記本上畫畫。

「嗨，馬可，你好嗎？」露西問。

馬可抬起頭，當他看到露西時，笑了笑。

「嗨，露西，妳好嗎？」他說。

「還不錯。」她說。她向窗外望了一會兒，之後說道：「跟我說說納森的事吧。」

馬可聽了很意外。

「你想知道他的什麼事？」他問。

「我也不知道，他都不說自己的事，他住哪裡啊？爸媽是做什麼的啊？你是怎麼認識他的啊？」她說。

馬可不知道要如何回答她，但他又不能把真相告訴露西。

他答應過納森的，他不能透露他爸的事，或是他在倫敦的生活。不過，馬可不擅長說謊，結果把事情抖了出來。

「很抱歉，露西，我不能說。」他說。

「為什麼不可以說？是有什麼祕密嗎？」露西問。

馬可臉紅了起來。

「是一個祕密囉。」露西說完，笑了起來。

「有什麼好笑的？」馬可問。

「你不能跟我說納森的事，因為那是一個祕密；我不能跟你說蘿拉的事，因為那也是一個祕密。」她說。

P.55

馬可看著露西，他想問蘿拉的祕密，但他知道露西一定不會説的，而他也不能跟她説納森的祕密。

「你為什麼想知道納森的事？」他問。

「這是祕密。」露西説完，又笑了一下。「你在畫什麼？」

「我在設計場景，還沒有畫好。」馬可説。

「我可以看嗎？」

馬可把筆記本遞給露西，露西看著他的畫。

「畫得很好耶，我喜歡。」她説。

「真的？」

露西開始翻閱筆記本，當她看到納森捧著碎掉的心站在舞台上的那張畫時，便停了下來。馬可看得出來她在注視著繪畫旁邊的「N 愛 L」這幾個字。

「喔，不會吧，她會不會誤以為『L』就是『露西』？」

「謝啦。」露西一邊説，一邊把筆記本遞回給馬可。

馬可不知道該説什麼，他怕露西難過，不敢讓她知道真相，所以就什麼也沒説。他確定露西應該可以從他的表情看出來 L 並不是指露西。L 是指蘿拉。不過呢，人有時喜歡自欺欺人，只看自己想看的東西。

P.56

「納森真幸運，能有你這樣一位朋友。跟我説説你的事吧，還是説，這也是個祕密？」她説。

「我啊，很簡單。我和我媽住在倫敦的南區，她是個警察。我爸呢，他住在曼徹斯特，所以我很少看到他。他們已經離婚了，我爸之後也已經再娶了，現在有他自己的家庭。你呢？你有兄弟姊妹嗎？」

露西並沒有在聽他講話，她心裡在想著納森。

祕密

・這個故事裡有哪些祕密？
・誰偷偷地在喜歡誰？
・你有暗戀的人嗎？

14. 鮑伯

P.57

第二週的第一個下午，鮑伯要所有參與演出的人到劇場舞台和他會合。這是他們第一次站上舞台，大家莫不顯得興奮。他們抬頭看看頭頂上的燈光，然後朝觀眾席上的空位望去，觀眾席上的中間位置坐了一個人，那是鮑伯。

「燈光！」鮑伯喊道。

劇場的所有燈光的瞬間熄滅，除了從舞台前方照過去的聚光燈。現場頓時一片鴉雀無聲，安靜了片刻。

「我要你們回想一下你們之前的試鏡，那時候我們請你們站起來介紹你自己，記得嗎？現在呢，我要你們輪流站在聚光燈前，用你自己的話來向觀眾介紹你的角色。我想知道你在劇中飾演哪一個角色，並請說明角色的內心世界，可以嗎？等你們準備好了……」

有片刻的時間沒有人站出來，之後蘿拉才走到舞台前方，站在聚光燈中。

「我的名字叫菲兒拉，我在一次意外中失去了部分記憶。我和我的孿生哥哥瑟貝俊一起搭船，後來船隻發生海難，我不知道瑟貝俊是生是死，他有可能滅頂了。在海難之後，我一個女子因為害怕落單，所以就男扮女裝，改名為夏沙力歐。後來我遇到了公爵。」她說。

P.58

蘿拉看著納森這時走進了聚光燈中。

「嗨，我就是公爵，伊利里亞的歐西諾公爵。我也是一位詩人。我第一次見到夏沙力歐時，覺得他這個人很老實，所以就讓他在我那邊工作。那時候，我很迷戀住在附近的奧莉薇，但她說她對我沒有意思，不過我不肯相信。總之，她就是不肯和我講話，於是我就叫夏沙力歐去找她談，為我說情。」

這時露西走進聚光燈中。

「他在說的人就是我，我是奧莉薇。我的哥哥剛過世，我沒有心情理會公爵。他是一個很自我、很愚蠢的人，我對他一點感覺也沒有。於是他就派了一個叫做夏沙力歐的年輕人來找我，我第一個反應是叫他離開。不過因為夏沙力歐長得很俊秀，我想我是喜歡上他了，而不是公爵。」

「很好！」鮑伯從觀眾席上叫喊道。

P.59

所有的演員介紹了自己的角色，也把《隨心所欲》的故事帶了出來。講完最後一幕之後，鮑伯來到舞台上，並請大家坐下。

「那麼，這齣戲的主題是什麼？」他問演員們。

「錯覺。我喜歡上夏沙力歐，而不知道她是女兒身。」露西說。

「欺騙。我女扮男裝。」蘿拉說。

「愛情。我愛奧莉薇，奧莉薇愛夏沙力歐，夏沙力歐愛的卻是我！」納森説。

「你們全都説對了！這個故事在講述人類在戀愛時所會出現的各種瘋狂想法和行逕，連這齣戲的劇名都具有瘋狂的意味。《隨心所欲》就是指『你想怎樣都行』。如果莎士比亞現在還活著，他可能會把這齣戲稱做《隨便啦》。」鮑伯説。

鮑伯模仿青少年浪蕩不羈的聳肩動作，説出父母們最痛恨的這個字「隨便啦」，於是引來一陣哄堂大笑。

隨便啦

• 在你們國家的語言裡，有什麼用語和「隨便啦」的意思相近？

在排演結束後，納森走過來和蘿拉講話。

「我昨天有 google 你。」他説。

「你説你怎樣？」蘿拉説。

「我昨天有上網搜尋你的資料。你知道全世界都多少人都叫做蘿拉・瓊斯嗎？」他説。蘿接沒有回答。「不過，我沒有找到你或是你的名人媽媽。」

「她換過名字」蘿拉邊説邊離開。

15. 納森，馬可

納森在跟馬可説他上網搜尋過蘿拉時，馬可説她有不可告人的事情。

「你怎麼知道？」納森問。

「露西跟我説的。」馬可説。他並沒有跟納森説另一件露西所透露的事情。

「我們星期一跟他們去松塢，搞不好可以發現她的祕密，找出她的名人媽媽到底是誰。」納森説。

馬可覺得這樣做不是很好。

「這是跟蹤，這樣做不好。」馬可説。

不過，馬可對納森是言聽計從。

星期二下午，在排演結束後，這兩個朋友便尾隨蘿拉和露西，一路從劇場走到國王十字車站。

納森和馬可常在電視和電影的偵探片中裡看到跟蹤的橋段，不過在真實生活中跟蹤起來要困難多了。他們在兩個女孩穿過尤斯登路時，差一點是跟丟了人，女孩差一點在國王十字車站裡消失了身影。車站內人潮擁擠，納森和馬可四處張望，沒有看到蘿拉和露西，之後才遠遠看到他們正走向第二月台。

「我們要買票。」馬可説。

他們走到售票口，買了兩張去松塢的

來回票。售票口的女售票員笑了出來。

「松塢不是地名，如果你們要去松塢製片廠，那就要買到丹漢的票。去丹漢的火車要去瑪麗蕾本站搭。」

「那第二月台的火車是要開往哪裡的？」

「皮特波羅。」她說。

P.61

「那請給我們兩張去皮特波羅的車票。」他說。他們很快走向第二月台，上了前往皮特波羅的火車。他們可以看到蘿拉和露西正坐在車廂的最後面。

「他們有看到我們嗎？」納森在火車離站時問道。

「我想沒有吧。」馬可回答。

半個鐘頭之後，他們看到蘿拉和露西下車，兩人於是又尾隨他們走出希金站，然後走上大馬路，一直來到蘿拉右轉的街角。

「接下來呢？」馬可問道，一邊看著蘿拉和露西兵分兩路地前進。

「你去跟蹤露西，我來跟蹤蘿拉，我們二十分鐘後在車站會合。」納森說。

P.62

很快地，納森看到蘿拉打開住家的前門，走了進去。

「爸？媽？我回來了！」她一邊喊道，一邊把身後的前門帶上。

納森站在人行道上看著她的住家。這是一個普通的兩層樓半獨立房子，前面有一個小小的庭院，還有一個車庫，車庫的外面停了一輛車子。「這看起來不像是電影明星住的房子，我們也不是在松塢，而且她爸爸還活著。」他想。

在這同時間裡，馬可跟隨露西走進一條窄窄的道路，道路的兩旁種有行道樹，立著幾幢獨棟的房子。露西在其中的一棟房子外停下腳步，她抬眼望了一下房子，馬可以為她準備走進屋子，不料露西卻突然變卦，繼續沿著道路走下去。馬可走向她家，抬頭向窗戶望去，看到裡面有一對男女，聽到他們正在大聲爭吵。「他們一定就是露西的爸爸媽媽了。」馬可想。他盯著房子看了一會兒，然後轉身走回車站。

「跟你說做這種事實在是不好吧。」馬可看到納森時說道。

「我們回家吧。」納森說。

兩個男孩在返回倫敦的一路上，什麼話都沒說。

真相

• 馬可和納森查出了露西和蘿拉的什麼事情？
• 他們滿意自己所查出來的結果嗎？
• 你想「跟蹤別人」這種事情好嗎？和夥伴討論。

16. 蘿拉，露西

P.63

在隔天的排演上，鮑伯要大家練習劇本的最後一場戲。

在戲裡頭，菲兒拉（蘿拉）喜歡公爵（納森），而這時候她的孿生哥哥瑟貝俊也來到了此地。瑟貝俊並未在海難中喪生，結果奧莉薇（露西）誤以為他就是夏沙力歐（菲兒拉反串的角色），於是要他娶她。當公爵發現夏沙力歐原來是女兒身（菲兒拉）時，才意識到自己是喜歡她的。

「等等！」就在即將結束之前，鮑伯喊了出來，「這是喜劇，不是悲劇！」

鮑伯看著納森，他今天演得很走樣，台詞丟三漏四的，而且一臉愁容。在他的角色需要向菲兒拉告白時，他表達得一點感情都沒有。

「納森，你是怎麼了？有人翹辮子了嗎？」鮑伯問。

納森注視著地板，心裡想的都是昨天的事情，心思根本無法拉回來演戲。

「這個劇本好瞎。」納森最後脫口說道。

「它當然很瞎啊，這是喜劇。」鮑伯說。

大家都笑了出來，除了納森。

P.64

「我想不透我為什麼會愛上她。她欺騙了我，她女扮男裝。」納森說道，眼神並未看著蘿拉。

「我也搞不懂我為什麼會愛上你，你個性陰晴不定，而且很自我。你五分鐘之前愛的人還是她！」蘿拉笑著。

納森這時抬起頭來，看到蘿拉伸手指著露西。

「至少我不會拿身分來欺騙別人。」納森對蘿拉說。

鮑伯這時感覺到情況不對勁。他要大家休息一下，離開房間，除了納森和蘿拉。

「你們兩個是怎麼了？」兩個人被留下來之後，鮑伯問。兩個人都默不作聲，鮑伯說：「我現在也要離開，留下你們兩個單獨相處。你們要把話講出來，把問題解決掉。我需要相信你們兩個人是相愛的。」

鮑伯走出了房間。蘿拉看著納森，她知道他心裡一定有很不爽的事情。

「出了什麼事？」她問。

「我知道你的祕密了。」納森說。

「你是在跟我講話，還是在跟菲兒拉講話？」她問。

「跟你。我在跟蘿拉講話，假設你的名字真的叫蘿拉的話。」他說。

「這當然是我的真名了，你到底想說什麼？」

「我知道你的祕密。」納森又說了一遍。

「什麼祕密？」她緊張地問道。

「你撒謊，你騙了大家。」

蘿拉把眼神移開。

P.65

「我不知道你在說什麼。」她說。

「你媽媽不是名人，你爸爸也還沒過世。你不是住在松塢，事實上根本就沒有松塢這個地方，這只是製片廠的名字。」納森說。

「你是怎麼知道的？是露西說的嗎？是露西說的，對不對？」蘿拉問。

「我是怎麼知道的並不重要。你為什麼要說謊？」納森說。

蘿拉惱羞成怒，轉身走出排演室。

露西這時正在走廊上等著蘿拉。

「事情還好嗎？」露西問。

「你怎麼可以這樣對我？虧我還把你當成我的朋友！」蘿拉氣沖沖地說。

「我是怎麼對你了？」露西驚訝地問。

「你少跟我裝蒜了！你永遠都不要再跟我說話了。」蘿拉說。

蘿拉沿著走廊走去，最後轉彎消失不見。露西不知該如何是好，她是應該追過去，還是去找納森談？她走進排演室，看到納森坐在角落裡，雙手抱著自己的頭。

「發生什麼事了？你和蘿拉是出了什麼問題？她是吃醋了嗎？」露西問。

P.67

「吃醋？」納森抬頭看著露西，「你這是什麼意思？」

露西在納森的身邊坐了下來。

「你有跟她講我們的事嗎？」露西問。

「我們的事？」納森問道，覺得情況更錯亂了。

「別擔心。我也和你有同樣的感覺。」她說。

「你怎麼會知道我是什麼樣的感覺？」納森問。

「我看到繪畫了，是馬可拿給我看的。」她說。

「馬可？你在說什麼啊？」納森這時才突然想起馬可的畫，他畫他捧著一顆破碎的心，心裡頭寫著「N愛L」。

「喔，不會吧，你以為我……」納森說。

他話還沒講完，鮑伯這時剛好走進房間，其他的學生也都跟在後面走了進來。

「各位，聽好了，我們現在再從最後一場的第一幕開始練習，請大家各就各位了！」鮑伯喊道。

納森不再多做解釋，不過露西聽明白了。「我怎麼會這麼蠢，L是代表蘿拉，不是露西！」她想。

露西衝出排演室，納森跟在後面叫著她。

「露西，快回來！」

17. 納森

P.68

當天晚上，馬可打電話給納森，但是納森沒有接。他不想跟馬可講話，「他幹嘛拿畫給露西看？」他自問道：「搞不好他也把我的祕密跟她說了，這下子大家都會知道我爸是誰了。」

「晚餐準備好囉！」賈桂向著樓上喊道。

納森這天晚上在餐桌上很安靜。在賈桂拿走通心粉碗、端上巧克力冰淇淋布朗尼甜點之際，爸爸在一旁盯著兒子看。

「這是我最愛吃的。」爸爸看到布朗尼時說道。

「這我知道，我是你的頭號粉絲，記得嗎？你的事情我知道得一清二楚。」賈桂說。

「我還以為你最愛吃的是土司夾蛋。」納森說。

「那是他最愛吃的早餐，布朗尼是他最愛吃的甜點，第 145 期的《擊峰》雜誌有寫。」賈桂說。

賈桂這時離開房間去打電話。納森正盯著牆發呆。

「要做全世界最有名的搖滾歌手的兒子，並不輕鬆啊。」他想。

你出名嗎？

- 你認為為什麼當一位知名搖滾歌星的兒子不是一件輕鬆的事？和夥伴一起討論你們的想法。

P.69

「『綠房』現在進行得怎樣了？你有認識新朋友，或是遇到什麼特別的人嗎？」爸爸問納森。

「你為什麼這麼問？」納森說。

「因為你看起來很鬱卒啊。來吧，納森，跟我說說。」爸爸說。

納森放下甜點小湯匙，做了一個深呼吸。

「爸，你別生氣喔。」納森開始說道，「我覺得你很厲害，真的，我是這麼覺得。只是，我有時候會覺得自己的存在好像是多餘的。」

「你繼續說。」爸爸說。

「在學校，別的小孩之所以想認識我，都是因為你。他們想跟我做朋友，這樣他們就可以跟我回家，看看我的名人老爸。他們有興趣的人根本就不是我。」

「不是每個人都這樣的，馬可就一直是你的好兄弟。」爸爸說。

「沒錯，我認識馬可時，馬可並不知道我是誰，所以我以前才會喜歡他，也很信任他。」

「以前？馬可是做了什麼事了嗎？」

「他把他的一張畫拿給一個女生看，結果那個女生現在以為我喜歡她。可是我並不喜歡她，我喜歡的是她的朋友……我……還滿喜歡的。」

「她朋友的名字是？」

「蘿拉。她跟大家說她是知名電影明星的女兒，我也相信了。我就想，因為我們都是名人的子女，所以應該可以成為好朋友。不過我後來發現她是騙人的。」納森說。

P.70

「哈！」爸爸笑了出來，「那她對你有一位名人老爸有什麼感覺嗎？」

「她不知道。我在綠房試鏡時，沒有跟任何人提到我或我爸是誰。我想憑實力進學園，而不是因為我爸是一位大明星。我就這樣做，結果我進學園了。後來我認識了這個女生，而現在呢，什麼事情都變得一團亂。」納森說。

「我跟你說說我的想法吧。我想你心裡很不是滋味，因為你很喜歡的人竟然說謊。問題是，如果你喜歡她，那她爸媽是誰就不重要。她說謊，有可能是因為她想讓自己不一樣，讓自己特別一點。你也是一樣，你想假裝成另外一個人。」爸爸說。

「那不一樣啊，我只想讓自己正常一點。」納森說。

「你本來就很正常啊，納森。就連我，我也是很正常的啊，你信不信？你想，人會因為出了名，就變得不一樣了嗎？」

「不會。」

「一定會有人是因為你老爸有名，或是你自己有名，才想認識你。不過，給別人一點時間吧，你很快就會知道誰是真正的朋友。這是我的經驗談啦。」

「那我應該怎麼做？」納森問。

「你自己知道怎麼做，」爸爸說：「不過首先呢，你可以先去幫我收email。」

忠告

• 納森的爸爸給他什麼樣的忠告？
• 你同意這樣的忠告嗎？
• 如果你是納森，你接下來會怎麼做？

18. 蘿拉

P.71

隔天早上，露西沒有來希金車站和蘿拉碰面，蘿拉於是自己搭車前往倫敦。「露西可能是搭早一點的班次，好避開我。」蘿拉想。她坐在火車上，望著窗外，她彷彿在窗戶的玻璃上看到了納森一閃而逝的面孔。

納森有可能真的喜歡她嗎？不過就算他喜歡她，現在大概也不再喜歡了吧。「但願我沒有撒那個謊。」蘿拉自言自語道。她戲演得很好，犯不著去撒那種謊。她不需要靠名人老媽來讓自己成功或是受歡迎。像納森，他是劇場學園裡人緣最好的學生，而他只是一個普普通通的人。

火車已經抵達倫敦，蘿拉望著窗外飛逝而過的房子。「不知道納森住在哪裡。」她心想著。

整個早上，蘿拉都刻意避開納森。她不知道要和他說什麼，也不知道要如何面對他，所以她早上在上熱身課程時，一直站在排演室的最後面。當課程結束後，她也假裝沒有聽到納森在叫她。

「蘿拉，我想跟你談談！」

她刻意鑽進學生人群裡往餐廳移動，

119

讓納森找不到她。後來，她走出劇場外面，站在街上等早餐的時間結束。在她準備走回劇場時，馬可剛好經過。

P.72

朋友

• 為什麼這四個朋友都在躲避彼此？
• 你有躲過朋友的經驗嗎？為什麼？

P.73

「嗨，蘿拉，你有看到露西嗎？」他說。

「沒有，怎麼了？」蘿拉問。

「大概也沒什麼吧，我昨天看到她氣沖沖地離開劇場，我想和她講話，她卻跑掉。我晚上就打電話給納森，但是納森不接我的電話。我今天沒有看到露西，所以就想……昨天是發生什麼事了嗎？」馬可說。

在蘿拉還來不及回答之前，鮑伯剛好出現。

「蘿拉，海倫夫人想跟你談談，就現在！」他說。

蘿拉沿走廊走下去，來到海倫夫人的辦公室。她很緊張，海倫夫人是要跟她講什麼？難道納森跟她說了我撒謊的事？還是露西發生了什麼事？她敲門，等著回應。

「請進！」海倫夫人喊道。

蘿拉打開門，嚇了一大跳。和海倫夫人一起坐在房間裡的，竟然是她的爸爸媽媽！

「媽？爸？你們怎麼會來這裡？」她問。

在他們還未回答之前，海淪夫人要

她先進門再說。

「很高興聽到你爸爸還在世。」海倫夫人笑笑地說，「不好的消息是，你爸爸媽媽都不知道你在這裡。」她拿起蘿拉第一天帶來的父母同意書，「我知道這份同意書是偽造的。」

「你為什麼不跟我們說呢？你為什麼要騙我們說你去參加泳訓呢？」蘿拉的父親說。

P.74

「因為這你們又不懂的。」蘿拉說。

海倫夫人笑了出來。

「我發現這實在令人難以置信。」她說。

「什麼？你指什麼？」蘿拉問。

「你媽媽對劇場可是很懂的，是不是，蘿絲？」海倫夫人說。

蘿拉的媽媽對女兒笑了笑。

「我想你一定會覺得很難以置信，我在你這個年紀的時候，也很想當演員。」她媽媽說。

蘿拉不敢相信。

19. 馬可，露西

P.75

難以置信

- 蘿拉知道了爸媽的什麼事？
- 你曾經發現過爸媽的另一面嗎？
  和夥伴分享。

「事實上，我也在綠房上過課，我
呢，就是在這裡認識海倫和你爸爸的。」
她繼續説道。

「爸爸？你也曾經想過要當演員？」
蘿拉説。

蘿拉的爸爸笑了出來。

「我不像你媽那麼會演戲啦，她真的
很有天分。」他説。

「你怎麼都沒有跟我説過？」蘿拉問。

「你從來都不跟我們聊啊，蘿拉。」爸
爸説。

「我們沒想過你也會有興趣，你的時
間都花在泳訓上，我們是這樣想的啦。」
媽媽説。

「你媽媽原本是要當明星的，不過她
認為組織一個家庭才是更重要的事。」
海倫夫人説。

「那你們怎麼會知道我在這裡？露西
跟你們講的嗎？」蘿拉問。

「你的朋友露西是完全清白的。」海
倫夫人説，「我第一次看到你時，就覺
得你很面熟。等到我看到你飾演菲兒拉
時，我就知道了。那時候，我便撥了電
話給我的老友，蘿絲。」

「所以接下來呢？我是不是應該離開
戲劇學園？」蘿拉問。

P.76

馬可在希金站下車，沿著馬路進入鬧
區，最後來到露西的家。馬可知道事有
蹊蹺。露西昨天為什麼要閃開他跑掉？
納森為什麼不接他的電話？海倫夫人為
什麼要找蘿拉談話？露西今天為什麼沒
來綠房？

馬可來到了露西家，不過他知道露西
現在不在家。他繼續沿著馬路走下去，
跟隨露西那天所走的路線。路的盡頭來
到一處公園，馬可於是走了進去。公園
裡頭有一些網球場、一些長椅和一個表
演台。馬可看到表演台的地板上坐著一
個人，那個人正在聽著 MP3。他走近一
看，認出來是露西。

「哈囉。」馬可低頭看著露西説。露西
一開始沒有聽到他的聲音，當她抬眼看
到馬可時，嚇了一大跳。

「馬可！你怎麼會在這裡？」露西一
邊問，一邊關掉音樂，「你是怎麼找到
我的？」

馬可在她身邊坐了下來。

「我爸媽在離婚之前很會吵架，那時我也有一個像這樣的地方。當我不想回家，或是他們又要開始吵架時，我就可以去那個地方。」他說。

「可是你是怎麼知道我住在哪裡的？」露西問。

馬可於是跟露西說了那天的事，說他們跟蹤她和蘿拉去國王十字車站，然後搭上火車來到希金車站，然後納森跟蹤了蘿拉，而他跟蹤了她。

P.77

「你們為什麼要跟蹤我們？」露西很生氣地問，「這樣很恐怖耶！」

「都嘛是納森的主意，人在戀愛時就會幹蠢事。」馬可說。

「我覺得自己根本就是白痴。當我看到你筆記本上的畫時，我還以為 L 代表露西，而不是蘿拉！」露西說。

P.78

「我知道，我應該跟你說清楚的，很抱歉。」馬可帶著歉意說道。

「那你為什麼不跟我說？」

「你看起來很開心，我不想讓傷你的心啊。」馬可說。

他們彼此凝視了一會兒，之後露西笑了笑。

「答應我，下次你就會跟我說清楚了，不要再有什麼祕密了。」露西說。

「我答應你。」馬可說。

「很好，所以呢，你現在可以跟我說你是怎麼認識納森的，還有他到底有什麼天大的祕密了吧？」露西笑了出來。

「這樣不公平。」馬可說。

不過，他還是把始末跟她說了。他跟她說，納森的爸爸是一個知名的搖滾明星。幾年前，他爸爸接到一通陌生人的來電，對方說如果不給一大筆錢，就要綁架他兒子。他爸於是報警處理。馬可的媽媽是警察，在警方尋線逮捕綁匪的期間，納森去他們家住了幾個星期。那時他們一起去上學，常常混在一起，但是納森對自己的家庭或是過去，一概隻字不提。他們後來變成了超級好朋友，當馬可得知納森的爸爸是誰時，真是嚇了一大跳。

「這的確是天大的祕密。蘿拉要是知道了，我真想看看她會是什麼樣的表情。」露西說。

「我們現在去倫敦吧，現在還來得及趕上劇場下午的排演。等納森跟蘿拉說他的祕密時，你就可以看到她的表情啦。」馬可說。

Part 3 演出

20. 蘿拉，露西，馬可，納森

P.79

首演當晚，海倫夫人把大家都叫到「綠房」（譯註：即演員休息室）。每一個劇場都有「綠房」，那是演員在開演之前或演出中途，等待上戲或是休息的地方。沒有人知道為什麼會叫「綠房」，有人覺得這個名字是來自房間牆壁的顏色，不過這間劇場的綠房是藍色的。

當海倫夫人和鮑伯走進綠房時，所有的演員和工作人員都鼓掌拍手。海倫夫人看著每一個人，笑了笑。

「今晚是一個重大的時刻，你們大家為此辛苦賣力，我知道你們的演出一定可以博得滿堂彩。你們個個才華洋溢，應該為自己所完成的事情感到驕傲。我們盡一切力量來支援你們，不過接下來就要完全靠你們自己了。等表演的序幕一開啟，我們的任務就結束了。」

P.81

馬可拿出筆記本，開始畫下這一幕。

海倫夫人說：「在各位上台之前，我還有一件事想跟大家說。我之所以要在綠房這裡跟大家說，是因為在這個房間裡，演員會回到真實人生的樣子。」

海倫夫人繼續說道：「在舞台上，你可以扮演公爵，扮演海難的倖存者，扮演丑角或是船長，不過在綠房裡，你們是真實的人，擁有真實的人生。有時

候，我們會希望自己的人生能像戲裡面那樣多彩多姿和完美，不過，我們的人生不是由莎士比亞所寫。我們人生的故事可能不盡人意。我希望你們能記住——在綠房裡的這個你，遠比舞台上的那個你重要多了，而你生活周遭的那些人，也比舞台上的其他人物角色重要。現在，出場吧，祝大家好運。」

蘿拉、納森、馬可和露西，他們走下樓梯，沿著走廊來到舞台。他們輪流從布幕後方看了一下觀眾，馬可的媽媽在那裡，蘿拉的爸媽坐在前幾排，納森的爸爸在忙著簽名，而露西的爸媽也答應休戰一晚，前來劇場。

「最後倒數，」劇場經理喊道，「大家各就各位，第一幕第一景就緒！」

「我們中場綠房間見啦。」納森說。

P.82

「好主意。」蘿拉說。

「還有誰很緊張的嗎？」露西問。

「我，我的手都在發抖，雖然我沒有要上台！」馬可說。

這四位朋友笑了笑。馬可最後又看了一眼他設計和繪製的舞台背景。納森踏上揭幕時要站的出場位置，蘿拉和露西在舞台的兩旁等待。他們聽到觀眾的聲音隨著暗下來的燈光安靜下來，在布幕拉起的前一刻，一片鴉雀無聲。納森走上舞台，說出他的第一句台詞：

如果音樂是愛情的糧食，
那麼就演奏下去吧。

123

ANSWER KEY

Before Reading

Page 6

a. Laura
b. Marc
c. Lucy
d. Nathan

2

Marc because he's holding a notebook.

Page 7

4

1. d 2. g 3. f 4. c
5. h 6. b 7. a 8. e

Page 8

5 b

Page 9

8

a. Will
b. Will
c. Will
d. James
e. Will
f. James
g. James
h. Will

Page 10

9

a. Well
b. It

c. Errors
d. Venice
e. Dream
f. Nothing
g. Juliet
h. Night

Page 11

11 a. F b. T c. T d. F

Page 16

For a place at the summer acting school "The Green Room".

Page 20

Because she looks into people's eyes before speaking and she speaks directly to everyone without looking at the floor.

Page 26

Marc introduces Laura to Nathan. Laura introduces Lucy to Marc. They say "This is..."

Page 38

Letters of acceptance.
They will go to "The Green Room" this summer.

Page 40

Her mother and father (she says her mother is a famous actress and her father is dead). Where she lives. She tells her parents she is at swimming practice.

Page 44

Learning how to act.
Adventure or new experience.

Page 49

Become their character.
The other actors they work with.

Page 56

Lucy's parents' arguing. Nathan's famous dad. Laura's real situation. Nathan likes Laura. Lucy likes Nathan.

Page 62

They don't live in Pinewood. Laura has a very normal family and her dad is not dead. Lucy has problems at home.

Page 70

Give people time to find out who your real friends are.

Page 72

Because of misunderstandings.

Page 75

They did acting when they were younger.

After Reading

Page 84

1. a. nervous, because of the audition
   c. guilty, because she lied to her parents
   e. stupid, because she was acting nervous
2. The theater.
3. Because she said she had a famous mother.
4. Lucy.
5. Because it was a lie and Lucy knew the truth.
6. Because her parents thought she was swimming.
7. Nathan. He couldn't sleep and he wanted to know more about Laura.
8. Nathan and Marc were in the kitchen. Laura was in her bedroom.

Page 85

9. Nathan.
10. He drew the picture of Nathan holding a broken heart.
11. They started with a physical warm-up session.
12. People spoke differently in the past and Shakespeare wrote in verse.
13. When she saw Marc's drawing in the coffee shop.
14. They had to introduce their characters.
15. They wanted to find out where they lived.
16. She ran out of the rehearsal room.
17. So they can come home and meet his famous dad.
18. They were also interested in acting when they were young.
19. He used to go to a similar place when his parents were fighting.

Page 86

1
a. jealous
b. Nathan told him to go
c. better
d. paper
e. bad
f. didn't want
g. wasn't

2
Laura lives a normal life although she pretends to have a famous mother. She thinks it will make her more special. Nathan's father is a rock star but Nathan just wants to be normal.

3
Lucy's parents argue. Marc's parents argued a lot before they got divorced. Lucy has a place to go when she doesn't want to go home. Marc had a similar place.

Page 87

4
a. Dame Helen, to the students before their first performance, in the green room.
b. Lucy, to Laura, when Laura forges her parents' letter enabling her to attend "The Green Room".
c. Nathan, to his dad, when they are talking about friendship.
d. Bob, to Nathan, when they are doing trust exercises.
e. Laura, to Lucy, when they are discussing about why Lucy went to the auditions.
f. Marc, to Bob, when he asks where Marc learnt to draw.
g. Nathan's dad, to Nathan, when they are talking about Laura's lie.

5
a. She's Nathan's dad's number one fan. She usually prepares their meals.
b. He works at "The Green Room". He has red hair and a red beard.
c. She's a police officer. She looked after Nathan when the kidnappers threatened to take him.
d. She used to be an actress. She decided to have a family instead.

Page 88

1
a. F b. F c. T d. F e. T f. F g. T

2
They stop pretending to be other people.

3
To be yourself and not pretend to be someone you're not.

4
love

5
They are both about people pretending to be other people and falling in love with the wrong people.

Page 89

6 c
7 a

Page 90

1
a. soulmate
b. fan
c. make-up
d. impression
e. heart
f. tragedy
g. set

2
a. on
b. up
c. up
d. out
e. down
f. in

Page 91

3
a. act
b. acts
c. lies
d. acting
e. lie
f. lying

4
a. left
b. have started
c. sent
d. was walking
e. starts
f. saw
g. felt
h. isn't

Page 92

1
a. C b. A c. C d. A

Page 93

2
a. 4 told
b. 2 received
c. 1 kidnap
d. 1 a lot of
e. 4 for
f. 3 couldn't
g. 3 great
h. 2 who

國家圖書館出版品預行編目資料

男孩女孩的夏日劇場學園 / Robert Campbell
著；安卡斯 譯. —初版. —[臺北市]：寂天文
化, 2013.9　面；公分.

中英對照

ISBN 978-986-318-142-2 (25K平裝附光碟)

1. 英語　2. 讀本

805.18　　　　　　　　　　102016001

作者 _ Robert Campbell
譯者 _ 安卡斯
校對 _ 陳慧莉
編輯 _ 安卡斯
封面設計 _ 蔡怡柔
封面完稿 _ 郭瀞暄
製程管理 _ 宋建文
出版者 _ 寂天文化事業股份有限公司
電話 _ +886-2-2365-9739
傳真 _ +886-2-2365-9835
網址 _ www.icosmos.com.tw
讀者服務 _ onlineservice@icosmos.com.tw
出版日期 _ 2013年9月 初版一刷（250101）
郵撥帳號 _ 1998620-0 寂天文化事業股份有限公司
訂購金額600（含）元以上郵資免費
訂購金額600元以下者，請外加郵資65元
若有破損，請寄回更換

〔限台灣銷售〕